# Samuel Bagster of London 1772-1851

SAMUEL BAGSTER 1772–1851

Portrait by J. Linnell 1850 reproduced by permission of
National Portrait Gallery

# Samuel Bagster of London 1772=1851

## AN AUTOBIOGRAPHY

SAMUEL BAGSTER & SONS LTD.
LONDON W.1

© Samuel Bagster & Sons Ltd. 1972
First published in 1972 by
Samuel Bagster & Sons Ltd.
72 Marylebone Lane, W.1

SBN 85150 000 5

Printed in Great Britain
by Ebenezer Baylis & Son Limited
The Trinity Press, Worcester, and London

# Foreword

I have read with great interest this Biography of Samuel Bagster, whose son, Jonathan, and grandchild, Anne, were the compilers of that beautiful book—*The Daily Light*—a collection of texts for every morning and evening during the year. *The Daily Light* was given to me by Dame May Whitty, soon after my eldest son, John, was born, and I have read it every day for more than sixty-two years. It is my close companion.

I read this life of Samuel Bagster with great interest; seeing in it the background of *The Daily Light*. The idea of the book was born in this splendid God-fearing family, Jonathan being the tenth child, and I feel the inspiration behind the book springs from the atmosphere of the family of Samuel Bagster.

How many readers, like myself, will enjoy this autobiography, and will be grateful to the Bagster family for their inspiring work—*The Daily Light*.

SYBIL THORNDIKE CASSON

# 1772 - 1779

One of the most direful and exciting incidents in the eventful series of Napoleon's wondrous course, which I remember to have read in a periodical of the day, is this: Napoleon, after obtaining a splendid victory over the enemy, in which action an awful carnage on both sides; after which, Napoleon directed a review of his army; that, in person he might have the opportunity, as the troops passed before him, to express his warm praise on officers and men, for their achieving so great a triumph; though gained at the expense of so much sacrifice of life. Near this great Commander, stood Colonel xxxx to whom the Emperor turned and addressed him "Colonel, where is your regiment?" "Sire! I am that regiment." The historian is silent as to the rejoinder of Napoleon to this pathetic answer of the Colonel; probably his regular practice of visiting the battle-field after a conflict, may have quenched in him the feelings common to our nature on witnessing such revolting scenes of carnage, but this anecdote is fixed on my memory, and, I narrate it, because to me were the question now put, "Where is your family generation?" my reply would be similar to that of Napoleon's Colonel, "I am that generation—" My father, mother, brothers and sister are gone—I alone (all one) am left—Not the carnage of war; but, the keen edged scythe of time has mowed down all and left me the solitary representative of my family.

I am now balancing the point, whether to begin with myself, or, my ancestry. I conclude on the latter, though I may have no materials for the boast of high ancestry, yet may the desire be rightly encouraged to dwell with satisfaction on our forefathers, who have consistently filled up their day with honour to themselves leaving a moral example to their descendants; and, in addition to the personal interest taken in individuals of the family stock, it is natural to an ingenuous mind to feel a warm interest in the localities they adopted as their home, and, especially so, when the same place of residence continues to be occupied through successive generations.

Gibbon, the historian, when employing his pen, as I am now affectionately doing, writes, "For my own part, could I draw my pedigree from a general or a statesman or a celebrated author, I should study their lives with the diligence of filial love." Perhaps the person from whom my family first traces its pedigree, though not a general, was qualified to be one, by his lofty bearing to a noble exile, combined with firm loyalty to his Sovereign, whose throne that exile came to usurp.

Tradition preserved in our family states, that prior to 1660 the family residence was in the Isle of Wight, that my great great grandfather James in or about that year, came to Lyme Regis, Dorsetshire; that he was in the Naval service, a lieutenant; that he married an inhabitant of that town on August 23rd, 1665; that on the landing of the Duke of Monmouth on June 11th, 1685, he was on the beach, and the barge containing the duke and his suite, not being able, because of the shingles, to come near enough to step on shore without getting wet, the lieutenant promptly stepped into the water, placing his knee for the Duke conveniently to step on, which he did, and, by a jump, landed on the beach dryfooted. The Duke politely thanked him, and said, giving him a familiar stroke on his shoulder, "My brave fellow! You'll follow me." "No, Sir! I have sworn allegiance to my king, and I will be true to my oath."

This tradition receives support from the fact, that the lieutenant, not being a native of the town, did not partake of their affection to the Duke's cause: had he been a native, he would probably have yielded to the general impulse to serve him, because he was a protestant, and was opposed to the Duke of York, brother to the king and next in succession to the throne, who was a bigoted catholic. The opinion has been historically stated, that every one of the town, capable of arms, joined himself to the invader's interest.

Our Naval progenitor, James, had two sons and three daughters, his first born was of the same name as the father, and, on the Duke's landing was eighteen years of age, and our tradition has left it uncertain, to which of these the anecdote applies, to the son or to the father, I am inclined to decide that the elder claims the honour, because the rank of Lieutenant could not be held by one so young as the age of eighteen, neither does the tradition state, that the son was in the Navy at all.

The second son of the first named James, named George, was my great grandfather, who, by the Church register was baptised on August 15th, 1674, and married to Joan Stocker on January 21st, 1703. She died on January 4th, 1776, aged 94 years. The fruit of this marriage was, five sons and three daughters, their second son, George, my grandfather, was born October 30th, O.S. 1708, baptised January 4th, 1709, and married to Alice Bonner, August 20th, 1730, she died in 1783 aged seventy-eight and he on October 27th, 1795, aged eighty-seven, leaving two sons and two daughters. The eldest of the two, my dear father and bare the name of his father, and was born July 19th, O.S. 1739, married my dear mother Mary Denton on December 8th, 1770. He died on December 24th, 1819, aged eighty years—My dear mother was born May 6th,

O.S. 1738 and died November 7th, 1823 aged eighty-five
years, they leaving five sons and a daughter living—
The writer of this narrative is their second son—Samuel
Bagster—

The locality of the pilgrimages of our ancestors is ever a
point of attachment to their descendants; and eminently
is it so with me—Lyme has its record in the history of my
country—The inhabitants are of note for their bravery,
even the women it is recorded shone as Amazons at the
siege of Lyme. The popular poem published in 1674
trumpets forth their fame—It bears the following long
and quaint title.

Joaneneidos or Feminine Valour eminently discovered in
Western women, at the siege of Lyme: as, well as, by defying
the merciless enemy at the face-stand, as by fighting against
them in garrison towns: sometimes, carrying stones; anon,
tumbling stones over the works on the enemy when they have
been scaling them; some carrying powder, others charging the
pieces to ease the soldiers, constantly resolved for generality;
not to think any one's life dear, to maintain the Christian
quarrel. Whereby, as they are commendations in themselves,
so they are proposed, as examples, unto others. [The above
forms a small 4° volume.]

The author, by his Title, intends honour to the Lyme
heroines; and, to lay a claim for his own share, by the
lofty quaint title—AEneis doubtless from Virgil's poem on
Æneas's travels after taking Troy; and thereto joining
Joan, in reference to that intrepid female in her noble
defense of Orleans against the English. May I be forgiven
in offering the conjecture, that my great grandmother was
named *Joan*, her parents intending thereby to evince their
estimate of the valour of Joan of Orleans—? She was born
four or five years after the publication of this book. Joan
is popularly known as the "Maid of Orleans—" She was in

consequence of her wondrous doings charged with sorcery, was condemned by the credulous and cruel judges, as guilty and was burnt alive May 30th, 1431, being then only eighteen or nineteen years of age—This legal murder, is a stain fixed immovably on the town, the judges and on the Duke of Bedford, the English commander, by his acquiescence—In my excursion to France, I visited the spot, in the old market place, where she suffered, and felt painful emotions standing on the spot where the revolting tragedy was acted—See Southey Book 1.

> She saith that God
> Bids her go drive the Englishmen from France—
> Curious they mark'd the Damsel. She appear'd
> Of eighteen years; there was no bloom of youth
> Upon her cheek, yet had the loveliest hues
> Of health with lesser fascinations fix'd
> The gazer's eye; for wan the maiden was,
> Of saintly paleness, and there seemed to dwell
> In the strong beauties of her countenance
> Something that was not earthly—Then cried she,
> "I am not mad—Possess'd indeed I am!
> The hand of God is strong upon my soul,
> And I have wrestled vainly with the LORD,
> And stubbornly, I fear me. I can save
> This country, Sir! I can deliver France!
> Yea—I *must* save the country!—God is in me;
> I speak not, think not, feel not of myself.
> HE knew and sanctified me ere my birth;
> HE to the nations hath ordained me;
> And whither HE shall send me, I must go;
> And whatever HE commands, that I must speak;
> And whatever is HIS will, that I must do;
> And I must put away all fear of man,
> Lest HE in wrath confound me."

The sculpter and architect have joined their talents in the

erection of this fountain and figure of Joan—The busy scene, to my English eye, was much increased in interest, by the active girls and women, all wearing a high cap of picturesque form—The newness of the costume of the women and my noticing that each one was unobservant of the figure and the erection; far otherwise with me; for, as I write at this distance, I renew my emotions and the following lines ran from my pen "abhorrent of the deed"—

> On closest search through Europe's bound
> Can men be found—can *one* be found,
> Who does not feel his spirit rise
> When Joan's fair figure meets his eyes?
> Be sure there never has been one,
> E'er since the direful deed was done.
> O ice-bound soul!—Not catch a spark
> Of sympathy for Joan of Arc!
> Flow, fountain flow, for ever flow,
> Though wheresoe'er thy stream shall go,
> Thy flowing stream can't cleanse the guilt
> Which here the bloody monsters spilt.
> Fountain! thy stream can't cleanse the place
> The deed deep stains the human race
> Black monument to man's disgrace.
> Firm granite wastes by Time's decay,
> Time's womb can ne'er produce a stainless day.

But to return to my personal history, which I began to introduce, by saying, that I was the second son of George and Mary Bagster.

Memory embraces the first links of life and brings remembrances of infant days, which, though somewhat indistinct and scant—yet are the germ of character—the chronicle of the earliest social feeling and observation; time may soon totally efface the recollection of my early days and progress through life, and leave a blank that never can be filled, but at present, many circumstances are as fresh in my memory, as though but the transactions of yesterday and I think my *earliest* impressions are the strongest—What a proof is this of the value of early instruction and moral influence—

According to my very excellent mother's report my birth took place on the 26th December, 1772 (for though present it has not any personal confirmation) however good Mrs. Henry's certificate of her attendance professionally (for then only females were assistants), and the register confirms the fact. I have heard, that my mother was disappointed that my birth was delayed one hour beyond the day of the nativity of our Saviour—At the next birth her wish was gratified; for, my brother William was born on Christmas day, two years afterwards. Between him and me, there was an actual contrast of person, his frame was muscular and large and his physical powers beyond children in general; but, feebleness of frame was the character of my existence; and, to this, probably I was indebted for a comfort that no other child enjoyed, to be nourished at my own mother's bosom, while all the rest were nursed by others—In subsequent life my attention and attachment to her, became more constant and tender, than any other of her children; nor was it interrupted or diminished, until our Saviour's words were shewn to be true, "A man will leave his father and mother and cleave to his wife."

The name of Samuel was given to me in remembrance of Mr. Samuel Hodges, who acted a paternal part to my mother, her sister and her two brothers—On the death of both their parents (which occurred during their childhood) Mr. Hodges (brother to my deceased grandmother) took the four children to his own home and adopted them as his own—He resided on Richmond Hill, where he had a kiln and manufactured bricks and tiles, and, in that occupation, excavated that vast hollow which now so painfully disfigures that charming scenery.

My mother sometimes amused her children with narrating the events of her girlhood on this hill and amongst them, especially remembered those of a noble family residing in the vicinity, the head of which was imbecile—The Earl of Portsmouth conspicuous by his rank and eccentricity, became eminently the object of notice to the youth in the neighbourhood. Several incidents of his ludicrous peculiarities, now present themselves to my mind; but, one only, will I mention, which will serve to exhibit the innocence and the features of his imbecility—The young nobleman was in his farmyard, when the pigs were making a considerable noise; he went to the sty and observing a silver spoon in the trough; he did, instead of taking it thence, ran to the servants, charging them to quell the riot, crying loudly, "the pigs are in an uproar, for, they have one spoon amongst them all to eat their supper with."

To this parental relative Mr. Samuel Hodges, my mother (who was the youngest of the four) and her sister were indebted for the dower received by their husbands on their respective marriages; and, their two brothers were provided for, by placing the eldest in business as a grocer, at the corner of Theobald's Road; and, the younger was apprenticed to a confectioner in Gracechurch Street; but, during his apprenticeship he died, having been so sadly ill used by his master as to require a public enquiry into the circumstances of cruelty and cause of death, which produced a severe reproof on his master—

The portrait of good Mr. Samuel Hodges is in the possession of my nephew Mr. George Bagster—

My first period of life was personally marked with all

the results of the feebleness from my birth; and, which,
by my frequent sickness and fractiousness occasioned no
inconsiderable trouble to my mother. Within this period,
I was committed to the care of Mrs. Hodder, who lived in
Islington, that I might derive benefit from the air of that
more healthful locality than home, it being in a crowded
neighbourhood and considered unhealthy—While under
Mrs. Hodder's care, the earliest incident my memory very
distinctly holds, was, an exercise of her tender sympathy
towards me, when a gathering fever made it evident, that
smallpox would follow; the kind woman, in a tone of
voice, which has *now* a melody to my ear, said, "You shall
sleep in my own bed tonight." I remember being put to
bed and the very tune she sang to soothe me (for she had
a nightingale voice) is fresh in memory. This pleasant
remembrance, proves, that a young mind receives a deep
impression when gentleness and sympathy occur in a time
of suffering. On my recovery afterwards, her exquisite
voice was not forgotten, again and again have I asked
and prevailed on her, to sing to me and not being wise
enough to know the words, I used to say, "Do sing me 'a
la ca visse' " and the favourite french pastoral song followed—Mrs. Hodder was the widow of a respectable
chemist, who resided many years in Newgate Street; and
was in the profession of the office of housekeeper to the
Apothecaries Company, from this office or duty, her
reliance for support rested. She had two sons and a
daughter, the eldest son had a club foot, and her daughter
was quite a cripple, both feet being so disfigured. The
daughter died in her girlhood.

While with Mrs. Hodder, my little drama presents an
occurence, which she afterwards often told me with
playful jeer, calling me her "little captain". Perhaps my
readers will not find fault with my pen for recording my

title to the honour; if they can discover no bravery in it, I assure them *I* was *then* satisfied with my claim to heroism. When persons were going to Islington from some parts of the town, the nearest way was to go from Holborn up Red Lion Street and Lamb Conduit Street, round the E. side of the Foundling Hospital wall, along a narrow lane, a sort of bridle road, with a bank and a ditch—This lane was considered dangerous (with reason I believe) after dark; and, females waited at either end, as the watchman with his lantern, travelled to and fro to accompany him, for the security of his protection. On one occasion, I was with Mrs. Hodder, waiting for the watchman; and, thinking it too long to wait, I said, "Don't wait Mrs. Hodder, you have a man with you". "Yes, my little hero", said she, taking me up in her arms, "I have a little man with me but I *must* wait for the watchman". This lane was then the occupation road, affording entrance to the several fields—fields and lanes no more, all are covered with streets and squares.

The way to the Brill, where my uncle and aunt Weston resided (Mrs. Weston, my mother's sister) was over the fields entering to the West of the Foundling Hospital wall, which fields were called the Long Fields. About a furlong to the west, stood a mansion for the Russell family, called Bedford House, the north front of which looked on to these fields. At the back of this front, was a good garden, which was bounded by a low fence, outside of said fence was a slope or wide ditch of stagnant water about 10 ft. wide or perhaps more, into which it pleased the public to adopt it as a well-adapted receptacle for the bodies of domestic animals—a canine and feline cemetery—and a variety of other filth. From this ditch a poor woman got some help towards her support by extracting from the jaws of the larger dogs, the teeth called canine teeth which, then, were used by bookbinders in burnishing the edges of books, but at this time agates have displaced the use of the teeth— The class of canine dentists are among the "Has beens".

These fields, called the Long Fields, were three, and on the foot path at the junction of the fields, was a circular turnstile and until the Brill was reached only one house was standing called "The Bowling Green". In a general way, it may be said these fields were lonely, and my cousin Charlotte Weston, who came over them to school every morning and returned home at *noon*, was stopped by a man and robbed of a new shilling and a silver thimble. General Oglethorpe, who died in 1785, used to shoot snipes in these three fields. To those who traverse squares and streets for miles without interruption, must be forever strangers to the contemplation, of one of my age, viewing contemplatively these broadlands covered with buildings, where, as a boy, I gathered daisies and buttercups, in which boy, proved to girl, and girl to boy, the love of butter clearly by the reflection of the yellow on the chin. The daisied surface of verdure is now Purbeck granite!

In Mrs. Hodder's residence, and, while under her care my health somewhat improved; and I went from her on a visit, and a long one it proved, to my mother's brother, Mr. John Denton at St. Pancras, who, after his resigning the grocery business, became superintendent of the brick, tile and chimney-pot manufactory of Mr. W. Weston, the husband of my mother's sister, and who resided at the other extremity of the manufactory, at the hamlet called, The Brill; which, with the public house called "Brill House", were the only houses on the plain, now forming the immense population, built on the estates of Lord Somers, Lord Camden and the Duke of Bedford.

After the death of good Mr. Hodges, Mr. Weston, who succeeded him in his business, left Richmond Hill, having, before his removal, married my mother's sister, came to Deptford to reside, and at New Cross built the now standing kiln, which has still "WW" worked in the brick front. Many years after when Mr. Weston died, which event took place at the Brill—, it was thought right as he had attended the service at the Independent Meeting House in Butt Lane, while he lived in Deptford, he should be buried beneath that place, there was he buried, with much funeral pomp, and the Rev. Mr. Mede the parochial clergyman of St. Pancras attended the funeral in his robes.

While on this prolonged visit to my uncle and aunt Denton, it was my uncle's duty to go at midnight, when the great kiln was burning, to ascertain, that the fire was of a right and equal power throughout its whole surface, if too weak at any spot, to see supplied the additional quantity of coals required in the fire beneath and if too strong in parts, to throw sand over the surface of the too free burning mass—The stoker, whose name was Thomas Trindal, a man of genuine kindness and of native ingrafted amiability—The faithful performance of his duty, was an indwelling principle with him, his employers knew his worth, and evinced their esteem. One evening my aunt yielded to my coaxing, to let me sit up *once* and see the great fire fed—I went with my uncle at the usual time and the sight can never be effaced from my memory—Three fires beneath, fed from the cellar below and were so long as to require a powerful arm to throw coals to the end but at the same time required the skill, which experience taught, that only such parts should be supplied as was necessary—This visit was for ever impressed on my mind, and, no wonder, especially, when to these three long chambers of fire below, was added, the broad face of the fire above—This circular fire appeared to me a child, terrifically large. Perhaps this scene though appalling in itself might not have been so deeply impressed on my memory, had not Tom Trindal's amiability won my love. Roused from indulged slumber by the fire side and brought into scenes so new and impressive—The night blowing brisk, the tempting offer was made to me by Tom, to eat a potato, which the kind stoker had roasted for himself in the ashes, and, so was it relished, that no subsequent palatial enjoyment, has equalled it or any one to compare with it, except I name a turnip I ate in 1814 on my visit to Beresford Hall—After this recital the reader will not wonder at the effect, I worried my yielding aunt to let me *always* go with my uncle to have the enjoyment of this hot potato—My wish was granted, and wet, dry, snow or frost, I believe my visit continued; and, that I never afterwards omitted to accompany him while on this prolonged stay and I actually longed for the return of this midnight adventure. After these burnings were completed and the red chimney pots were removed from the kiln and placed in the packhouses, there was found on several of them, a shrinking of the clay and fissures, not cracks, which were to be filled in, this was done with Suffolk cheese and brick dust over, which gave them a good face and a sounding ring when struck. It was a pleasurable employ to rasp these firm cheeses for good tempered Tom Trindal to use. This kindhearted young man (about 25) had always ready for me when I came to the kiln with my uncle, a large potato well roasted in the hot ashes and some salt in an oyster shell, and I was never weary of this luxurious food.

Some years after, I enquired about the kind fellow, who had given me so much juvenile enjoyment, and learned

*Note:* I was about four years old, when my great grandmother died. She was married to my great grandfather GEORGE on Jan. 21, 1703 and she died on Jan. 4, 1776, aged 94 years. Her maiden name was Joan Stocker.

the sad information, that no one knew what had become of him—A guess at his fate may be gathered, by what I once witnessed, while at my uncle's. At the time of this long visit, the war with France and America was in full activity and the Navy at this period to be hastily furnished with mariners, which was effected by forcible impressment of every youth and man that could be seized—The practice adopted, was, for a Lieutenant and eight or ten powerful lion-hearted men to form, in common language, a press-gang—Then, was it legal, to seize any one under thirty years of age that they could find; and the Navy required hands so much, that these gangs were numerous and active so as to create a general dread of being snapped up. The sad treatment of the impressed, to prevent their escape, was always close and too often rigorous.

But to my story—It was an uproarious scene I witnessed at the kiln, which arose from this prevailing fear. The men were busy "drawing the kiln" removing the burnt pots and tiles briskly, to prevent adhesion, as they cooled, on that account I believe, they were always removed when hot, so hot, that injury would be done to the man's hands but that they passed them so rapidly from one to the other, that they had not time to burn them. A most spirited and animated scene; and, just at this period of common and united energy, a loud voice of warning was heard, "The press-gang is coming." There was no need to repeat it—At the first sound of this awful sentence, every man fled to hide himself, leaving the property to its fate. On the occasion which I witnessed, the outcry was not founded in the fact, it was a hoax by some unfeeling witling —What I saw ending in a hoax, was however afterwards acted in reality—Good kind-hearted Tom Trindal, fled away with others, but sad it is to record, was never again heard of—his end no one knows; but, it is, that he was impressed and that he perished either in war, or, the hardships of compulsory sea service and the close restraint, contrasted with former freedom and muscular employment in the open air. My uncle expressed his esteem for the man's character, and regret for his fate; but I lamented it as a catastrophe, as no less than the loss of a friend!

In connection with this scene of Tom Trindal's hospitality and potato roasting, an event occurred worth recording amongst other incidents of this period—Not unfrequently destitute men and boys would request to enjoy nightly shelter in Trindal's warm dominions, which was seldom refused. One night heavy continuous rain, following days of a like kind, the water of the river Fleet, which conveys away the surplus water from the large Hampstead ponds and the water from the high lands to the North of London, had flowed down faster than the channel, with obstructions in it, could allow the flood to pass, the river consequently overflowed its bounds and spread desolation all around. That night two poor boys had obtained permission to spend the hours of darkness before the fires in the subterranean coal reservoir; and it proved their death; for the flood rapidly *filled* the base in which they were reposing not conscious of danger and so suddenly and so high did it arise, they could not escape; it extinguished the burning mass above, scattering the red hot chimney pots and tiles in ruinous overthrow. That night I did not sleep at Uncle Denton's but at Uncle Weston's at the Brill (the two residences a short furlong distant) and I was roused from my sleep by voices crying loudly for help, all I could make out was, "Two boys are drowned." As soon as possible the maid servant went down to learn the cause of the uproar and when she got near to the bottom of the stairs, she stepped into water and by the sudden surprise dropped the candle and in her sudden fright, arising from the cold water and darkness, screamed aloud, "I am drowned". The top of the flight of stairs, I should before have told my readers, had a flap that covered the whole, which was bolted above to secure the residents from burglary, a precaution really needful in that remote thinly inhabited district; the rise of this heavy flap hastily, in its fall, added to my alarm, not knowing the occasion of the noise. Speedily lights were obtained, all the family being roused, and from a window we learned the full particulars. The spot thus inundated was known by the name of "Pancras Wash" because in much rain not infrequently flooded but to the extent now in recital, never took place before—The little river then, was a clear ever-flowing rivulet of five or six feet wide and about a foot deep, unless when swollen by long continued rain—This little stream passed through my uncle's ground for a short distance and was one of my chief delights with the knees of my breeches tucked up to dabble in it, with a paper fleet of boats—This clear stream, *now* forms a great sewer of filthy contents and flows under Farringdon Street into the Thames at Blackfriars Bridge; through which it ran uncovered just before my time, and, when covered, became Fleet Market—This market also is removed and Farringdon Street is the name it now bears.

The solitariness of this outskirt of London was such, that after sunset it was dangerous to pass and repass to and from London, and dangerous to reside there—I have above named the precaution of a flap which shut over the head of the stairs and bolted above, and for additional security, my uncle had two dogs, which were let in to the kitchen at night, to give notice of danger, and a large Newfoundland dog, named Cosar, guarded the garden side of the house, being allowed to be loose at times and always loose at night—his end was ominous, one morning this fine animal was found dead and his body swollen. Not long after Cosar's death, three men attempted to force an entrance, by cutting the shutters of the kitchen window, the very room where the two dogs were loose and placed as guardians but both were quiet, the thieves had by art allayed their natural ferocity—The men were however interrupted in their acts by a woman living in a cottage at the back of the premises calling out, "Don't steal my ducks". The woman's voice awakened my cousin William Weston Junr., who passed through the room in which I slept (which was over the kitchen), and opening the window and looking out, he saw three men busy breaking in below; without shutting the window he ran back for his fowling piece, which was charged and again looking out saw them at a little distance, and, at the moment a cloud passing away, gave the light of the moon, and he fired at them. The next day drippings of blood were traced to the dry ditch at the boundary of this first field from the Brill and there more blood was seen, but, beyond, from that place, no blood was observed, probably therefore it is, that the injured man in the ditch, tied up his wounded limb— The ditch where these men relieved, as was supposed, the man wounded by young Mr. Weston, had on its bank a hedge, which margined a road then in use and which is now nearly the site of the very handsome road that stretches between King's Cross (then called Battle Bridge) to Paddington, known as the New Road. This public way is indebted for its beauty to an incidental circumstance, much talked of at the time; and the result of which has been since, and ever will be, a cause of gratulation to the public, and especially to the affluent inhabitants of the palatial residences of the gentry of England. Had this handsome fauxbourg, been a long line of houses cuddling in close, the entrance to the Regents Park, Portland

Place, &c, would be lost, but now, the whole is appropriated. When the committee of the Common's houses was
sitting in discussion on the Bill to form this road, the
harmony of opinion was not broken on any point during
the progress of discussion, until at its close the question
came under consideration, "at what distance shall the
houses when built be kept back from the path?" The
question came into the form "Shall ten or fifteen feet be
the distance." On that point a difference of opinion
seemed near to force the committee to decide by the
chairman putting the question, by a division of numbers
to settle the point—While this was under close argument,
a member, not of the Committee, came in to the committee
room and the proposition was made by the chairman, and
approved by all, that he should decide the question; he
refused to arbitrate, if bound to the bare question whether
ten or fifteen feet—he claimed to name another distance
if he chose, to this the Committee pledged themselves to
sanction and he at once named fifty or sixty feet, I forget
which, and thus the present road skirted with handsome
houses and passing between gardens, is the result. Before
this act was obtained some houses had been run up close
to the path which remain, as a foil to the pleasing ornamental consequences of the above sagacious decision.

An incident of my youth, which happened just about the
time of which my narrative tells, arises in my mind while
speaking of the New Road, and will establish the exact
topography of my spring days. I was on a visit at my uncle
Denton's and my brother George, was on a visit at my
uncle Weston's (for he was a mighty favourite with my
aunt which I was not). One day he came and spoke in an
undertone to his cousin Samuel Denton and together they
went out without me, and evidently on the sly. My
curiosity was awakened and my wit was sharpened to find

out their whereabout and at length after wide prowling, I discovered them in one of Mr. Rhodes's fields, bathing in a pond. I was boy and George was lad, a little man in company with his cousin, who was a little older. As soon as I discovered them I proposed to have a dip too and though not so old yet as naked as they were, was about to get into the water, they said, "You little chap you'll be drowned" and threatening to beat me if I got in, drove me away. *The spot* where this took place can now be seen, in consequence of the two houses which were built over the place of this pond, facing Judd place, having sank—I have as often as I passed through the New Road, looked at those two houses lower than the rest of the line of houses and thought of my boyish days and doings, the pond and the bathing!

Before or about the completion of my seventh year, my dear mother took a lodging at St. Pancras for the summer season at a Mrs. Heavisides, a short mile from my two uncles' residences. That and an adjoining house were the first modern houses for perhaps a mile around. The house was close to the old church at St. Pancras; it was then a fine open country. By the road side the house stood but between it and the road, was a two room cottage of antique build and which perhaps a Tudor prince's eyes had seen. The front parlour window looked on to a wall at the back of the cottage, composed of stone hewn and rough, brick and fragments cemented with clay, bare evidence of frequent reparation from many generations. The public path to the churchyard was between this venerable wall and the iron railing in front of Mrs. Heaviside's house. The cottage and wall restricted the view from the parlour floor; but, from the one pair windows, the scene was worthy of praise; at the distance of a moderately wide field a stately row of full grown unlopped elms were seen with all the grace of growth that tree exhibits and before those rich elms, a field of beauteous verdure, in which was a moderate sheet of water, much adorning the landscape and as a whole was a picturesque look out that is not often found in a near suburban spot— and then not to be despised—The venerable church too was near, with a lofty hedge surrounding the burial ground. The antiquity of the hedge was established by a grotesque large oak pollard tree, companion to the old cottage for some centuries, and one broad headed pollard willow.

On one occasion, I believe on my mother's birthday, May 20th, a party of juveniles were invited to spend a happy day with us. My uncle James Bagster's children and Tristram Bailey, the only child of Mr. and Mrs. Bailey of Holborn, completed the party. Tristram was a girl of overflowing spirits, the life of every active feat. All had arrived the day before, to have a full day of happy sport and on beds and mattresses spread over the floor—In one room we slept and no little amusement did our resting place produce. My mother had enough to do, between breakfast and dinner, to prepare us all, with our buoyant spirits, suitably clean and fit to appear at dinner time— We were however ready rather before one, the proposed dinner hour. Being ready before one, Tristram proposed for us all to walk in the adjoining churchyard, until dinner was ready, which my mother cheerfully granted and out we all went in an exhilarated flow of spirits. Presently one proposed as the rain drizzled that it would be high fun to get into the broad crown of the low pollard willow for shelter (though really it afforded none) and no sooner named than approved and as soon carried into effect, by the aid of a tombstone and a wooden railing, the stronger helping the weaker and Tristram best of all, there we all were when sought for to come to dinner but in such a pickle by wet and the green surface of the willow that we were direfully bedaubed and merry Tristram was drest in her best frock which was spoiled. We had stayed there long beyond the dinner hour, the servant not observing us, had returned and reported we were not in the churchyard. At length we went in and my poor mother was in utter dismay "too angry to show anger". "How could you do so foolish children!" was all she said but the day was lost to comfort or pleasure by this foolish though childlike love of adventure.

Mr. Wm. Bailey of Holborn (Tristram's father) was brother of Mr. Robert Bailey of Chard, Somerset, who married my father's sister "Betty Bagster"—The high esteem Mr. W. Bailey and my father had for each other has but few parallels in ancient or modern records, their intimacy and confidence in each other personified the brightest portraits of pure friendship, they were a very David and Jonathan. The very closest subsisted too, between Mrs. Bailey and my mother and when death removed good Mrs. Bailey, my mother mourned with a long and grievous mourning, to such depth was her sorrow, that her health was severely affected. One brilliant display of Mr. Bailey's genuine friendship to my father was charmingly evinced by his heroic conduct in a season of deep affliction. In 1777 or 1778 my father was seized with a putrid fever, of a most malignant character, wherewith he was confined to his chamber fifteen weeks and though attended by Sir John Jebb, the general practice, even in his reputed skilful hands, was so erroneous, that additional force was given to the malignity of the fever and it became imminent danger to be near the sufferer—Mr. Bailey braved the danger—regularly attended to my father's affairs, kept the account books, attended to the correspondence, even to some neglect of his own business and at the risk of his life, nobly and continually gave his friendly and valuable aid—A debt that should not be forgotten and which can never be paid.

At this summer lodging, which my mother occupied for several years, occurred two events whereby my life was placed in danger—probably both these incidents did not occur in the first septennial era of my life, one may have more right to an after period, during a school summer vacation, but I name them together. My brother William and I were angling in my uncle's brick field, in one of the great excavations from which clay had been taken, with our little rods, crooked pin and fragments of a worm, I drew out a stickleback in full season, rich in nature's colouring, and bawled out, "I have caught a cock salmon" (for such the name in juvenile nomenclature) and to make this prize secure and lest it should struggle from the pin, I stepped forwards to catch it in my hands and placing my foot hastily in a hole in the slippery clay, fell into the water; William full of his jokes, moved not to my aid, but laughing said, "A fine cock salmon indeed!" These broad and deep excavations are always sloping from the edge to keep the sides from falling in upon the diggers and the danger was that when falling in beyond the brink, the slope of slimy clay guided the unheeding one un-interruptedly to the bottom, where, by the force of un-obstructed descent the feet sticks in the miry clay and to arise would be impossible; which had been the case in two instances, the two boys who were drowned did not rise until means were applied to recover their bodies—I however succeeded in getting out on terra firma.

My other escape is as memorable—I accompanied my uncle Weston one morning to Mr. Norton's, a renowned brewer in Gray's Inn Lane, and while they were engaged in the transaction of their business, I traversed the brew-house. On being called to accompany my uncle on his return home, I was on the first or upper flat of the brew-house, from which was a descent by steps straight down to the door, without a bend—I, full of boyish bounce, deemed my ability equal to slide down these steps, holding part of the rail on each side, to give me an impulse—I sprang off but not clearing the lintel of the door, struck my head and was rolled into a mash tub of draining grains close at hand, which happily however was not hot enough to give me any discomfort, had my fall been two hours earlier my pen would not now be recording this provi-dential deliverance.

An incident apparently trivial, but which became important in its domestic bearing, made me, though a child in my fourth year, a principal actor—A young woman named Esther Ellis, applied to take the place of domestic servant and after a conversation with my mother declined entering the service on finding children were part of the family—As she was going out, Hetty (as we afterwards called her) many years after informed me, that I took hold of her hand, looked in her face and said, "I love you." These words from me a child, won her heart, she turned back, went in again to my mother engaged in the service and her abode in the family was more than half a century. When this faithful servant died, above sixty years subsequently to this event, she bequeathed the savings in our service, amounting to £300 stock, amongst the grandchildren of her master and mistress.

This aged and esteemed servant, was buried in St. Pancras burial ground, the eldest son of each family branch followed her to her burial place; about thirty yards from her grave is the tombstone of a lawyer, on which is sculptured an eulogy, that thousands have read;

and, perhaps, few of the thousands have denied the praise
nor deemed the satire inapplicable—

> Here lies one, believe it, if you can!
> Who, though a lawyer, was an honest man,
> The gates of Heaven, to Him were open'd wide,
> But they are shut, to all the tribe beside.

I regret, who does not regret, that the name of this "one
of a thousand" whose monumental eulogy has attracted so
much attention and more regret do I feel that an impression of professional delinquency so prevails, as to support
and justify the satire. This honest practitioner of the law,
was probably a Roman Catholic, having the words
*Requiescat in pace* beneath two sculptured cherubins. St.
Pancras is a favourite burial ground with persons of the
Romish faith. The recording stone is of some antiquity
as seen by its shape and antique form of letters. The grave
yard officials from generation to generation seemed to
have regarded this memorial with attention and respect.
The tombs around are much more modern, it bears clear
evidence of a remote period, the mouldering of the granite
by time and weather could not produce such decay in less
than centuries. Probably it bear this record before the use
of our impressive burial service—I have listened oft in my
boyhood age and felt a solemnising and perhaps a latent
dread of death, when the surpliced clergyman solemnly
pronounced dust to dust, and, on repeating the words,
the sexton officially standing by the grave, with the spade
in his left hand, and with a handful of earth in his right,
prepared to drop it on the coffin lid, which returning a
hollow sound, gave an impressed effect to the solemn
words and a sepulchral sensation unto mourners and
spectators and to each emphatically said "Thou also art
mortal".

But to poor Hetty just committed to the dust, I will return to record the *only* unkind thing I remember of her, it made a deep impression on my mind at the time and seems to give another proof (if proof were needed) that youths have, perhaps, unknown to themselves, a code of moral laws, a balancing of right and wrong—Circumstances in themselves trivial and which might be expected to be soon forgotten, are retained for years and the reasonings of the boy become the reflections of the man. The incident I am about to relate, took place when at home for the holidays from Northampton school. I went into the kitchen to give a message to Hetty, or to warm myself at the fire and saw one of our skittles on the fire beneath a saucepan—I experienced such a painful rush of violent anger and sorrow at her apparent heartlessness, and was so taken by surprise, that I stammered, and was unable to express myself. All I could get out, was, "How could you do it? How *could* you do it?" over and over again. Probably I estimated the wrong too severely, but it then seemed to my judgment, an evidence of a want of kindly feeling, or, even of moral sense, and the said skittle, skulked in my memory, and too often claimed domain, when Hetty with all her sterling qualities came into my mind. Who is there amongst the sons and daughters of Adam, that can pretend, on every occasion, throughout his whole life to have preserved a faultless conduct—Alas poor Hetty, that a spark from a wooden skittle should have burned a tiny hole in her fair mantle of praise!

Thus I close this first period of seven years—The family at this time consisted of my brother George, now the eldest (surviving two daughters who died in infancy); myself, the second son; William, before spoken of; and my sister Mary, the third of that name—The youngest son

John—Denton was not born till the month of June of the first year of my second Septennial era, of whom more will be said. After the birth of John—Denton, my cheerful father on an enquiry, "How many children have you, Mr. Bagster?" commonly replied "I have four sons and each son has a sister."

It is not easy to conclude one such period of life and enter on another, without awakening varied thoughts and feelings—it is a period of the rough and the smooth mingled, which has a direct bearing on the future stages of this mortal journey. The deep influence of early impressions on the future life arises from the mind being more susceptible and tenacious. This age is disposed to admit of copying examples near, without consideration, as the tender creeping plant clings to the nearest object for support.

A train of reflection presents itself on the entrance to a second stage of my life, having this peculiar stamp, it was the first movement towards a separation from my parents, to qualify for a total departure from them to enter the wide world.

# 1779 - 1786

The Second Period of my life began December 26th, 1779, with such feebleness of constitution, that I seemed as needing a staff to support me, nor had I perhaps as much advanced in the elements of learning, as I should have done at this age had my ill health not have been a drawback. While on the visit to Mrs. Hodder and my uncle Denton, no means had been employed to instruct; and indulged as I was, I had fallen into a habit of lisping unchecked, which so spoiled my pronounciation when reading, that my small capabilities appeared worse than they really were. My only instruction up to this period of my life, was in those intervals of time I lived at home, at a Dame school in a first floor, behind the New Church in the Strand. This Dame was a clever managing mistress, who kept the juvenile assembly of girls and boys in tolerable order, and did her arduous duty well. She was I believe a manumitted slave, not very dark, but rather a tawny coloured complexion and bore the name of Cosar, which was, either the name of her father or the name given to her on her manumission.

Mrs. Cosar was by all respected, and by her little pupils treated with reverence, "Yes Māām" and "Please Māām," were the tone of the children's addresses. Several years after I met Mrs. Cosar in Holborn and greeted her, and it pleased me to observe her face expressed content and her dress respectability.

The time was now come when it was determined by my parents that I should go to a boarding school, and the school selected was that of the Rev. John Ryland, A.M. of

Northampton, a choice I never regretted. The school was large, about ninety boys. When I joined the mass, I did not for a long time mingle with them—I did not seem one of them, being the youngest and carrying still the egg shell of the nursery in my timorous manners; and the shock of this busy scene would have probably broken my spirits had not the English teacher of the young, who was also the writing master, taken me under his wing. My father engaged him to shew particular kindness to me, giving him a compensation for so doing and faithfully did he fulfil his engagements. I could not eat animal food at this time, my dinner being usually bread. Sometimes in the hustle of a meal, it was my lot only to get one piece of bread and I have frequently left the table not half satisfied, and, even at the best supply at the dinner meal, my frame needed some help between the hours of one and eight o'clock, when the supper time came of bread and cheese. Mr. Hague, the usher alluded to, every afternoon when he left the schoolrooms between four and five o'clock, kindly told me to be near the Buttery door and there my attendance was punctual—Mr. Hague would be at the bread store and bring me half a roll or something of that kind and Miss Stott (the daughter of Mrs. Ryland by her former husband Captain Stott) used now and then to put a boiled egg into my pocket, thus, by these auxiliary supplies I got on tolerably well. To the long continued sympathy and supply afforded by the kind conduct of Mr. Hague I owe the establishment of my health and future comfort in after life, even to the day I now use my pen.

The school was of celebrity, and justly so, Mr. Ryland was assiduous in improving mental talent when it appeared and several men became eminent for oratory and scholarship by the education and training imparted there.

A short period before my entry, Dr. Ryland of Bristol

and the renowned Robert Hall, had left the school. The classical master at the time of my entrance was the Rev. George Dyer, a man of much reading and considerable erudition, but sadly lacking the talent which invites and fixes the attention of pupils and none made advances under his tuition. His bearing was repulsive to boys, though I consider he was in natural temper mild, and desired to be courteous. He had an infirmity too that as a teacher made against him, he was so short sighted that he held a book when reading only two or three inches from his nose and when the boys of his class stood before him, they grinned and made him a butt for grimace and fun. The pranks the lads played are rife in my memory but I see no profit in here recording them. I was never under his tuition. Mr. Dyer left the orthodox faith and adopted Unitarianism, which probably was the cause of his dismissal. He subsequently gained a livelihood by his pen. He wrote a history of Cambridge, was the editor of Valpy's edition of the Latin Classics in 149 volumes, and was a political writer. The Holcroft, Thelwall, Godwin and others, were his associates, and they have floated on the life current into the lake of oblivion.

Before Mr. Dyer resigned his scholastic employ, a Mr. Clarke took the Mathematical duties; and after Mr. Dyer left, Mr. Clarke took the classical department also. Mr. Clarke possessed very excellent qualities of mind, there was an adaptation in his natural disposition to teaching, which was very beneficial and the boys progressed under his tuition. He preserved his station with dignity, though without austerity or severity. My whole remembrance is to his credit notwithstanding one sad error he was guilty of, which remains in vigorous remembrance and can *never* grow pale and be obliterated— I refer to his most barbarous treatment of my brother

William—The case is notable—Though the censure my brother deserved is fresh in its full degree, I consider his punishment to have been greatly beyond the fault for which he suffered.

The narrative is—Hermann Witsius Ryland and my brother George were partners in a garden against the wall of the play ground, as some other boys had—In that garden were scarlet runner beans trained by strings against the wall, which flowered in luxurious abundance, to the admiration of all—The lower part had pods fit for the table. We had a pair of pigeons, which had two young ones. These had been killed to eat with these beans, the servant having engaged to dress the pigeons and the beans for supper that night, to be eaten, be it told in a whisper, in our bedroom. We early arose in the morning to pluck the beans, when lo! and behold! the pig boy had neglected to feed the pigs; in consequence they had broken out or jumped over the gate of the sty; and had, sad to tell, eaten up all our beans, as high as on the stretch they could reach. We witnessed their delinquency as soon as we entered the play ground and with speed drove them away. This was a true cause of mortification but the pigs were blameless, they obeyed the *lex necessitatis*. Our anger prevented us from reasoning, but at once we called up the other boys in our room to avenge our loss. Nimble feet and excited minds soon joined in an attack on the poor pigs. We hunted them from side to side with all the missiles we could command. *All* were energetic, but it so happened that my powerful brother, too often thus unfortunate, threw a cricket bat with such force, that the back of one of these little pigs was broken. Whereby our improper revenge was exhausted but the early morning, because of this accident, became the topic of everyone's tongue. Mr. Clarke soon ascertained that the blow which broke the back was William's act, and it so happened, that Mr. Clarke heard of it as he was entering from a walk with his usual walking stick in his hand; and as he reached the stairs which led up to the school room, we came in, and his eye fell on my brother William, whom he seized and beat with a severity and continuance I never before witnessed. The effect on my brother's person was hideous and called forth general commiseration—bruised over all his person, his sufferings were severe. This hasty and revolting cruelty was the effect of sudden passion, he should have remembered all were equally to blame—It is due to Mr. Clarke to say, it was an exception to his general conduct, but such an indelible impression did it make on my brother's mind, that after an absence of eighteen years in India, the *very first* enquiry on his arrival in England was, "Is that cruel Clarke alive?" And, to me, the effect prevented me from sending my sons to the school which he conducted at Enfield with great credit.

Hermann Witsius Ryland, the youngest son of our good tutor, went to Canada appointed by Lord Spencer, Secretary to the Governor, in which high office his duties were performed honourably for several years and on his death left a name in high respect.

The foregoing narrative should not convey an impression that severity was the mode of management at Mr. Ryland's school, by no means, the four-and-a-half years I was there I saw but two boys whipped, and that punishment was inflicted for running away from school. One boy whose parents lived at Pershore in Worcestershire enticed his bed mate, whose parents lived at Chatham Dockyard to abscond and they left together. They rose very early, ascended the wall bordering the play ground and, jumping from thence into a lane, made their way to the Angel Inn, where they hired a chaise for Newport

Pagnell (I think fifteen miles), to which place they were carried; on their arrival, they felt the awkwardness of their position; these unreflecting boys had only a few shillings in their power, when they had joined their funds. Not daunted, they started into the town to sell a pair of silver buckles worn by one of them and were directed to the house of a jew dealer. The Israelite was an honest man (as I have found many), he easily discovered their character and bought the buckles at a full price and they left his shop rejoicing at so good a sale. The Jew followed them to the inn, told the landlord what he suspected and on entering the inn the landlord who accepted all their money as the fare and put them into another chaise, as if for Woburn—The landlord returned the money to the jew and got the buckles—he ordered the boy to drive to the school at Northampton, and they did not discover they were returning back until they recognised the well known Queen's Cross, a mile or so from Northampton. They loudly called to the post boy, who had been ordered to be deaf, they then tried to get out of the chaise but the clever postmaster had put them into a chaise, which had a bolt outside which prevented the opening of the door in the usual manner, and thus these two adventurous boys were returned; and that before they were missed, the arrival of the chaise was the first notification of their absence.

These two boys before being punished, were brought to a trial "by their peers" as Mr. Ryland called it. Before the assembled scholars the boys were arraigned, defended, and by a jury of boys, declared Guilty, and the presiding judge passed the sentence to be whipped—and the enticer, as more guilty, to be more severely whipped—as the chief occasion of the other's crime. They were publicly whipped before all the scholars. They stood in the centre of the inner school room, in proper trim to receive their sentence, while Mr. Ryland made a speech and read chosen portions of scripture and when the words were read "spare the rod, spoil the child" the stroke was repeated. The punishment, as to its pain, was trivial but its length and solemnity made it heavy.

Another case of discipline arose of a very different character. A boy lost a cake and a shilling, which were taken from his box. Mr. Hague, the English Usher, adopted the following eccentric course to discover the aggressor. He metamorphised himself to appear as a conjuror. He wore a wig and seated himself in a corner of the room adjoining our long eating room, which had a door from thence and another door across the room, nearly on the opposite side. The pseudo-conjuror had a pair of globes before him on a table, and wore spectacles with broad brims. By the alone glimmering light entering in from a circular hole in the shutters, we could but obscurely see the woeful figure in the corner. Around the fireplace two strong chalk lines were drawn; we were told to tread exactly between them, the toes or heels were not to touch either. Thus, having placed ourselves, one after the other we were directed while so standing between these lines, to touch a kettle put in the fireplace, which, as we were told when the guilty person touched, a white cock therein, would crow and thereby the conjuror would discover the pilferer—one by one we entered: as each went out by the other door, his finger was examined to see whether the kettle had been *really* touched. Not many boys had entered when it was announced, the thief is discovered. The kettle had been so blacked that it could not be touched without marking the finger, it followed of course, if a boy came out with a clean finger he was chargeable as guilty, because he had feared to touch the kettle. Happily for the credit of the whole, the clean-fingered boy did confess his guilt and stated that the key of his box opened the box from whence the cake and the shilling had been taken. This contrivance carries with it no approval to my mind, though ingenious and successful. In schools of high character, there is generally felt by the tutor a solicitude to improve and expand a mind that predicates greatness—and my worthy schoolmaster was in one instance grievously wrong. One of the boys of tender age manifested extraordinary talent and Mr. Ryland paid a quixotic attention to him. This boy's precocity soon exhausted his physical powers and he died in early life. The plant perished by forcing it to bear fruit unseasonably.

Mr. Ryland was intense in his desire to implant patriotic and protestant feelings in the bosoms of his scholars. On November 5th the morning was engaged in reading from Rapin's *History of England* in folio, the account of the gunpowder plot, and in the evening, we were not discouraged from turning our pence into squibs and crackers, or clubbing to buy blue candles or rockets.

Another trait of the good man I will state—one autumn morning, he called up the whole school to see the departure of the swallows, which had clustered in surprising numbers on the roof of the building. His presence and zealous manner of explaining their migration has made this departure of the swallows a frequent occasion of bringing my worthy tutor to remembrance when seeing the summer visitor skimming the air with unwearied wing.

My readers are I am persuaded not weary of the traits in Mr. Ryland's character. He held his talented friend the Rev. James Harvey in profound esteem while he lived; and his memory after death was so precious that it might truthfully be said, he was enthusiastically fond of him. Under the influence of this love and reverence Mr. Ryland took some of the boys to see the church and the pulpit in which the "Great Harvey" had laboured. I believe not a single boy entered into the seraphic reverence of his amiable tutor; certainly I did not, for, as soon as the sexton had opened the church door, I hurried up the aisle and was gaping about, perhaps only wondering at the reason for taking so long a walk, but whatever was passing in my mind or whether my mind was inert or not, I know not; but, suddenly I was seized by the powerful arm of Mr. Ryland, who picked me up by the collar of my jacket, and then, with a jerk on a tomb-stone, saying, "Now boy for ever remember, for *ever* remember, you have had the honour to stand over the ashes of *James Harvey*." A poet would say,

> "He felt in his transported soul
> Enthusiastic raptures roll."

The Rev. James Harvey who was the author of *Theson and Aspasis, Meditations in the tombs*, etc., died on Christmas Day 1758 about twenty years preceding this visit to his church. My tutor wrote a book he entitled, *The Life of James Harvey*, a volume of nearly 500 pages, which exhibits such eulogistic fervour, that it may be deemed rhapsodical, and, notwithstanding it exceeds the limits of proper praise, the features of his powerful mind are seen on every page. His ardour of esteem has carried him near to absurdity. His learned but less vivacious son, the late Dr. John Ryland of Bristol, in reverence of his father's literary fame, purchased and destroyed the copies of the work when they came into his hand.

Many eccentricities manifested by Mr. Ryland in his mode of tuition and manner of preaching are present to my memory but omitted, not being strictly appropriate to my present purpose, but this pleasing truth I declare *confidently*, that on no occasion could the hearer doubt the purity of his motives; his one aim, the eternal benefit of those who listened to his instructions. I owe to him a high tone of moral feeling impressing on my mind; I believe, by his own *peculiar* manner of conveying instruction. The reader will perhaps like an instance: he when walking through the school, wearing his usual flowing camblet gown, on seeing a boy sitting listlessly at a desk, supporting his head by placing a hand on each cheek, went to him and with the tail of his gown flapped the boy rather smartly saying, "Do not sit idling here, go read or play, you are working for the devil". This is in harmony with Watts in his charming hymns for children:

"So Satan finds some mischief still,
For idle hands to do."

Mr. Ryland was most mild in his government, personal chastisement was hardly known, a sentence of reproof commanded the wished for rebuke, at times he could raise his voice high enough to "move the tiles": it was like a stentorophoic voice, as through a tube, and at the same time capable of every gradation until it was less than a whisper, and then it would arise with a soft euphonic tone, till it assumed its natural pitch again, all which was in harmony with his ardent character of mind, his tall stature and constitutional energy of action. Not in contempt or scorn was he by his scholars called "Boanerges". The complete sway he had over the scholars was without an apparent effort, it owed nothing to the fear of chastisement, his power to ensure obedience had great similarity to the manner in which our great naval hero Nelson displayed his controlling influence. I owe the following anecdote, illustrative of it, to the late gallant Sir Thomas Masterman Hardy, whom I knew from midshipman to admiral. On one occasion, Lord Nelson and Captain Hardy were going ashore in the admiral's barge at Plymouth, one of the sailors was under the influence of liquor or some untoward fit of bad temper had seized him; but, talk he would and would not keep the stroke of oars. His Lordship spoke to him, he did not desist, again he was spoken to warmly, but still he was not obedient. His Lordship then went to him and with a light buff glove, which he had been swinging in his hand, struck him with it in the face and said, with a Nelson authority, "Remember for ever you've been struck by your Commander!" It is not necessary to say the effect was complete—

Thus Nelson, thus Ryland ruled.

I will return for a few lines to his pulpit talent—His manner and sterling matter made his preaching popular, both with the vivacious and the sedate. Every word he uttered came warm from his heart and few persons could be inattentive nor listen without advantage. Occasionally he would illustrate and strengthen his argument by strong comparisons and contrasts; he was preaching in Dr. Gifford's pulpit (Dr. G. being present) his subject, the extensive erudition of the Apostle Paul, the evidence of which were manifest by his writings and oratory, and designing to give a deeper impression to his diffuse description of St. Paul's mental attainments, he said, "he was in person small, his jewel of soul was held in a poor casket"; "He was mean", here he paused and said "mean, *mean*" "as mean as", all which time his mind was evidently seeking a thing sufficiently mean to convey his idea of the inferiority of his body to his mind—then came the climax—"As mean as your little Dr. there" looking at Dr. Gifford sitting in his own pew. Dr. Gifford hastily arose from his seat, opened the door of his pew and then with gentler thoughts resumed his seat.

While mentioning Dr. Gifford's name in connection with energetic preaching, I will narrate an anecdote of him which took place in my early days. I must not have been seven years old, for it was August 24th, 1779, when the incident occurred. There was a very crowded assembly to hear the Rev. doctor preach a sermon on the day commonly by protestants, called "Black Bartholomew Day". The bloody deeds of that day were awful, very many thousands perished by the assassins in the dead of night by the King's authority, his command was woefully and cheerfully executed. The soldiers began the slaughter at the midnight tolling of the great bell, and in their midnight murdering of families, some escaped from their beds in their night clothing, hoping if it were possible to find a shelter and their lives be spared. The monarch was in a balcony watching the unclad fugitives who were fleeing from slaughter and he deliberately taking his aim, "just", said he, "as if I were to shoot that boy in the gallery window", putting his arm out and assuming the attitude of firing a gun at me. The shudder to me was great, for I was but a little brat put up into the window seat. What a dismal remembrance it stamps on the mind, for beside this numerous destruction of the protestants, the queen, the infamous Catherine de Medici, sent the head of the aged and excellent Admiral Coligni to the pope, who directed a grand Te Deum of praise on the execution of this atrocious event.

Dr. Gifford died in 1784. My father was one of his executors. He bequeathed many coins and things of antiquity and of intrinsic value to the British Museum, and he bequeathed his library and his invaluable Bibles to the Baptist College in Bristol.

I have placed the portraits of Dr. Gifford and the Rev. John Ryland in my sitting room, they bring pleasant remembrances of the past; and, the pleasure is increased by the latter wearing the cauliflower wig, as he wore when I was under his tuition and the portrait taken about the same period. Dr. Gifford's portrait is a copy of the portrait in the British Museum.

Mr. Ryland's mode of preaching I will further notice: on one occasion when preaching on the want of Christian fortitude in the cause of God (I was present) he took occasion to remark in confirmation of his views, "Were I at the London Coffee House (where he resided on his short visits to London) and began to speak of Jesus Christ, at once the current of conversation would cease and silence at first prevail, soon one to another would remark, in a whisper, 'I wish our conversation had not been interrupted'. Gradually the sentiment would be more openly spoken, all joining in the censure, and by degrees one would say *softly* to his neighbour, 'turn him out', then others joined in the cry 'turn him out'." The ardent preacher then rose by graduated strength of voice, from a smothered whisper, rising to its full power ending in a loud shout "turn him out". Persons passing must have drawn the inference, there was a tumult within and a refractory person was to be expelled.

There is now before me a memorandum of this worthy tutor's opinion of the proper education of the young— Some shall follow, because I here close my record of his school. He says:

I am convinced by long experience in the instruction of youth, that much more may be done towards furnishing and adorning the human mind, in the early part of life. It is a grievous thing to consider how we are suffered to waste seven or ten years in learning little more than mere words, whilst the improvement of the understanding and the reason, is most entirely neglected in most schools in the kingdom. The minds of youth are happily vacant of the cares and business of life; they are very susceptible of ideas of all kinds, provided you propose them in a simple and familiar manner, and avoid everything that is abstract and remote from sense.

Arithmetic and Geometry are exceedingly useful and important sciences for youth, and they may be taught in a more pleasing and insinuating manner than they usually are. Everything should be mixed with pleasure and familiarity that belongs to youth. Arithmetic can never be enough taught, it deserves more attention than is given to it. Geometry, or the doctrine of extended continuous quantity, including the consideration of lines, surfaces and solids.

Next to divinity and history this is certainly the very best science in which youth can be instructed. It has a prodigious tendency to fix the attention, to strengthen and enlarge the mind, to improve the memory, to teach clear ideas and form a habit of just reasoning. It is surely the best logic that was ever invented for the use of mankind.

I am very sure that all the parts of philosophy may be taught in the most easy and familiar manner, if schoolmasters had but public spirit, good humour and condescension.

The reader will indulge with an episode on the science of numbers:

Last week a young friend paid my family a visit, with his newly married wife, and remembering his employ had been tuition of youth, I asked him if he had had his attention called to No. 15, as the philosophical number. He had not—I then drew this diagram:

$$(681, 735, 249—15)$$

| 6 | 8 | 1 |
|---|---|---|
| 7 | 3 | 5 |
| 2 | 4 | 9 |

and asked him to solve the problem—to place the nine

figures in the squares so as to produce 15, which counted from top to bottom or from side to side.

My young friend then asked me if I was acquainted with the singular arithmetical problem that the addition of all figures terminate in 6. As is below exhibited:

$$1+ 2+ 3= 6$$
$$4+ 5+ 6=15= 6$$
$$7+ 8+ 9=24= 6$$
$$10+11+12=33= 6$$
$$13+14+15=42= 6$$
$$16+17+18=51= 6$$
$$19+20+21=60= 6$$
$$22+23+24=69=15=6 \text{ and so on to any}$$

number. Arithmetic admits of many amusing problems.

The talented and amiable author of the Memoirs of Robert Hall which are attached to the collection of his whole works in six volumes, alluding to that gifted man's education being in part at the school of Mr. Ryland, while he remarks on his advance in Latin and Greek, is silent on the moral and intellectual influence I have above presented. Had the excellent author personally known the abiding influence of such teaching, as Mr. Ryland's had, he would have concluded Mr. Hall left that seminary brimful of noble sentiments and deeply indebted to Mr. Ryland for opening and directing his intellectual powers; a training which gave through life bright evidence of its benign and noble control.

Much do I regret that I was removed so early as at ten years of age, and, no less regret, that I did not profit more, but, with these regrets, I am thankful the good impressions which I did receive, are indelible.

My readers will call to pleasurable remembrance the account of Mr. Bailey's sublime friendship, he had one only child, a pleasant girl of native cheerfulness, named Tristram (her mother's maiden name) who was at Mrs. Trinder's school in the market square, about half a mile or less from our school.

Mr. Jones of Stanhope Street had a son at Mr. Ryland's school and my father had three sons in it.

The three parents agreed to travel together on horse-back to see their children. My father and Mr. Bailey were strong men and accustomed to horse exercise and were well mounted, but Mr. Jones was a citizen unused to riding and rode a hired worn out horse. As may be naturally expected poor Mr. Jones was dreadfully jaded while Mr. Bailey and my father ended their journey fresh and in good spirits. Mr. Jones did not rally, he went to bed and passed a painful restless night and could not arise in the morning and a visit from the doctor gave much uneasiness to his fellow travellers, he stated his case to be imminently dangerous and, an express was des-patched to Mrs. Jones to hasten her visit or she would not see her husband alive, but whether she arrived in time or not, my memory fails to settle.

After Mr. Jones' melancholy death, hastened or pro-duced by his visit of love to his son, his son continued at the school and when finished, he was educated for the medical profession and became an assistant to his maternal uncle Dr. Thomas Arnold of Leicester, a practitioner of high repute for his successful treatment of the insane. Samuel Jones subsequently practised as a surgeon in the Navy, the pay was inconsiderable, not more than adequate to appear respectable. This condition my father was desirous to improve and my father's natural disposition and habit was—to be forward to serve a friend, and towards this young man he felt especial sympathy, he being bereaved of his parent, as it were, in his company;

and often he lamented he could not serve him; when one day the subject on his mind as my father was returning home after "attending change" this thought arose—I will see Mr. Goulburn, the Secretary of the Treasury, I do not know that gentleman but I will make an effort to see him, it costs only the time and the trouble. My father obtained an interview and made his request known. The result evinces that his open attractive and frank manner struck this great official. My father said he had no pretensions to claim this high favour but yet he hoped to obtain it. Mr. Goulburn said, "Give me his name, I do not think it can be done, but, if done, it will appear in the next gazette, and if you do not then see it there, you have no hope from me." In the gazette to my father's high delight appeared Mr. Samuel Jones, who thereby obtained an improvement so considerable that his half-pay was nearly equal to his full salary before. My father's pleasure was as great as his success was extraordinary.

My early departure to a distant school considering that my constitution was tender, was probably influenced by the fact, that the habitation of the family was to be changed while I was at school the first half year. Our removal was to Beaufort Buildings having heretofore been in Fountain Court two doors from the much spoken-of Dr. Kitchener. The change to this larger house had filled our young minds as a matter of extraordinary importance and greatly we longed to get home to see the new house.

This first return to home from school was in many respects to me enduringly memorable. Tindal pithily says, "Memory is the great keeper or Master of the Records of the soul, a power that can make amends for the speed of time, in causing him to leave behind him those things which he would carry away, as though they had never been." Memory has been to me a faithful "Keeper" of the circumstances of this era of my life. My heart was gladdened and my spirits flushed on this my first return home from school for at that time of life and state of health nothing could be a substitute for the associations of home. No one was young enough to be my companion there, so that my imagination was egg-full of the happiness of home.

The boys who had parents resident in London or whose homes were so situated as to require them to pass through the metropolis travelled to town in four chaises closely packed. At Kings Cross (a cross erected by Edward I to honour and remember his beloved and faithful Eleanor) all turned out to bid farewell to Northamptonshire and clustering round the cross gave as loud huzzas as each could produce. The whole joyous group gave the reins to the most exuberant feelings of joy. A perfect contrast by the bye is the passing it as we return to school!

In one of the chaises our tutor usually travelled. The cauliflower wig was heating and troublesome to the wearer and it was entrusted occasionally to one of the boys to carry on his hand and being so closely packed the wig could only be carried outside the window, a spectacle that would have given materials for jocularity had a Bunbury or Cruickshanks happened to have seen the cavalcade.

After a wearisome drag through Woburn Sands we arrived fatigued at the Castle and Falcon in Aldersgate Street (then kept by Mr. Dupont a celebrated wine merchant). The parents and other friends of the boys had come for them for my mother was very much beyond her time and my brother and I until my mother arrived amused ourselves by climbing over the large bales of wool which were under a lofty shed piled high. When our dear mother arrived, in a hackney coach to fetch us and our school boxes, we flew down and were soon encaged to our great satisfaction. The coach proceeded without interruption through St. Martin's le Grand, Newgate Street and the Old Bailey, but when we assayed to fall into the line of carriages on Ludgate Hill, our way was obstructed by a multitude of people in lawless uproar; The cry to the coachman "Hat off", "Shout no popery". Our driver was not to be driven, he was mute and his hat seemed to be nailed to his head, and the outcry increased! We were however saved from further insult by the discreet provision of my mother, who had brought with her a piece of ribbon of the popular colour which she pinned to a white handkerchief and waved it out of the window apparently with glee, and huzzas rent the air, our road was clear which enabled our sturdy coachman afterwards to boast, "I did not take off my hat to the vagabonds". With the interruptions of the unusually crowded streets we arrived safely to the top of Beaufort Buildings. "Go to No. 13," said my mother. "The soldiers will not let me," the man replied. Truly we could not for there were so many soldiers as to *fill* the street. The purpose of their assembling here was to protect Mr. Kitchiner's house and Mr. Heron's, both papists and who had received threatening letters. The former lived by the water's edge and the latter, a grocer of eminence, lived in the Strand.

The soldiers were there until the rioting ceased. Were it within my purpose, I might narrate the awful calamities caused by the lawless rabble that then assembled, inflamed and led by Lord George Gordon. I will restrain my pen from everything but those which engaged my personal attention and of which some circumstances will be stated hereafter.

At length we were escorted and helped by a soldier, who, by his officer was directed so to do; we and our school boxes got in; and, silly, impatient boys as we were, ran up stairs, before speaking to my father or anyone, to see every room in the new house, but, feel our keen disappointment—we were told not to enter the two pair front room, as Miss Burnaby was in it. All the rooms in the house (such is human nature) were unsatisfying and we felt discontented, because *that* room could not be seen. For some days this exclusion continued, a vexation to us and every time as we passed, endeavoured to peep in if the door was ajar—we saw nothing to be good, while this "Mordecai" was in the way of our full survey of the house.

Miss Burnaby, was the daughter of Sir William Burnaby, and had for several years, boarded and lodged with the preceding tenants of the house, and my parents felt indisposed to take possession of an apartment where she was happy; he was unwilling to interrupt her former habit of life. Miss Burnaby had a rich aunt, on whom she built the expectancy of ample means at her decease. The aunt occasionally came to take her niece out for a drive in her carriage; joyful to us was the sonorous sound of the practised footman's tatatat thunder at the door, we having formed our plan at one of these times to see the room. The lady was drest and ready prepared and the carriage drove off. Watching for this event, before the carriage was twenty yards from the door we were in the room. We gazed around eagerly painting on our minds everything therein. The mantle shelf struck our full attention, for, thereon were figures of animals whimsically moulded into grotesque forms and of all colours, except the natural hue. At the corners stood a grim heraldic lion, with square mouth full of appalling teeth—*Les dents de Lion!*

> Grotesque! nor lines, nor looks, nor shapes,
>   nor features true

To nature's form—false colours shed a hideous hue. I had courage to take down the monster-lion nearest me and my brother took down the monster nearest him and when we were both satisfied with the sight, we exchanged our lions; I put his lion on my corner and he put my lion on his side, by which transfer it occurred, that the lions did no longer grin at each other, as they did when we entered; but, when we left the room, they were placed back to back. We stepped out briskly and were soon again in the parlour, no one knowing we had been in the room, and felt mightily pleased at our activity and success.

When Miss Burnaby arrived back from her drive, she soon discovered the lions were back to back, altogether wrong for such ferocious creatures. With violence she rang the bell for Hetty, to know who had intruded into her room: "I am a lady born, and, though I do live in a single room, it is no justifiable reason that my privacy be thus entered. I feel slighted—I cannot bear it! I cannot bear it. It is bad enough not to be rich, but such intrusion I cannot bear." Then she bitterly cried. Hetty positively assured her no one had been in her room in her absence. We kept silent while hearing the story of her complaints. My mother sent to her by Hetty, her compliments, and she was assured no one had entered the room. This message produced the climax. To Hetty she said with anguish, "Look at the Lions! Look at the Lions! I left them face to face and now they are back to back. I *demand* to know who. They could not move themselves."

In consequence of this "Much ado about nothing" it became a family proverb, when grief was in excess, and the cause of grief unimportant. Cheer up! It is only one of Miss Burnaby's lions.

Another word about this lady: she spent her whole time in reading novels and romances and actually wrote a novel called, *Isabinda of Bellefield* which I printed many years after in three volumes and the edition was all sold. At length her aunt died, and she, as expected, became opulent, but the change of life disagreed with her and she died within the year after leaving our house.

An accident about this time happened, in itself of no moment, yet gave first birth to a feeling of some importance; until that incident, I regarded my father as faultless, as a model of perfect wisdom. I considered every reproof or direction as unquestionably right in judgment, whether pleasing to me or not. The slight change that took place in my mind was but a juvenile reflection and might have been expected to be of a transient impression but it remained and deepened and was influential, when myself a father. The incident took place in this my first or second return from school.

There is a practice very common with boys, to form arrows made of a short stick of light wood, with a strong pin's head driven in and the point out and adapted for flight by a slit at the opposite end and paper pushed down the slit. The use of it was to throw it at a mark, or, merely throw it to stick in any woodwork. Accidently or rather say carelessly throwing, the arrow struck a large engraving of the feast of Belshazzar and broke the glass of it. My father was *very* angry with me and the strength of his anger, that it would cost 15*s*. to replace it—the picture, and this he sternly repeated. The thought presented was—then my father weighs the fault at the high price of the glass, whereas my mind told me the fault would have been as great, if the glass had been only 15*d*. but the price of the glass was all that was alleged as the fault. By the way this play is personally dangerous; my then young neighbour Kitchener, afterwards the Dr. Kitchener of culinary celebrity, lost an eye by a young companion throwing one of these arrows into it.

Dr. Kitchener being named I will insert an anecdote or two of him. When in after life I was at his house in conversation, he looking suddenly at his watch, said, "I must go down to my evening devotion." This he spoke so lightly that I considered it nothing private, said "Shall I go with you?" "O yes if you like." Then from the drawing room we descended to the parlour, wherein was an organ of considerable power, to it he sat down, and with all the keys open, played *Non Nobis Domine*, and accompanied it with all the energy of his powerful sonorous voice. When this his evening devotion was finished, I took my departure. The doctor is of great culinary renown; he began his career in the study of this *science* by collecting authors who had written on this *important* subject, from Apicius to Mrs. Rundel. These advocates for good eating were not few—they exceeded in number the entire Royal regiment of "Beefeaters". As the yeomen of the King's guard appear well fed, the popular name seems appropriate and the corruption of the word beaufittier is forgotten. The duty of these yeomen is, to attend to the side-board on Royal festivals. From this digression I return to Dr. Kitchener and his Collectanea. From these advocates for obesity, he selected the choicest rules to be observed in cooking and eating and published the result of his researches in a work entitled *The Cook's Oracle*. In the humorous preface to this work he informs the reader that he formed each instruction "spit in hand" and that there was not one preparation he had not tasted. In furtherance of this *national benefit*, he gathered a "Committee of taste" and my *honour* I will not conceal I was a member of it. On a late occasion of meeting to the epicurean feast, the Doctor as president sat at the head of the table with a cabinet or nest of small drawers, at his elbow; I presume, containing different spices and aromatic herbs, to give the very relish his experienced palate approved. He did not open his cabinet once during the repast. I conclude my reader desires to know my opinion of this entertainment. It is soon told—it was anything but satisfactory, the dinner was slowly brought in, the viands chilled and to be eaten off cold plates. It lacked the comfort of a single dish with a warm plate and dear domestic associations. It was my last visit.

What a mighty chasm between the Father of gastronomical philosophy by Apicius, in the reign of Augustas and Tiberius and the author of the *Cook's Oracle*; the former aspired voluptuously to lofty and expensive costly delicacies for the opulent at no less an expense than £2,500,000, the latter embraced the million and taught the manner to dress a cow heel or shin of beef to form an aliment piquant and relishing.

Noble art! to give insipids savour.

And to give to nice a richer flavour—*see* Dr. King. Dr. Kitchener has favoured the public (aye generations yet unborn) with the result of his palateal experiments in a compound of ambrosial herbs, now selling under the title of "Dr. Kitchener's Zest". His ideas of human enjoyment were the gratification in luxury of food and the indulgence of the delights of sense and the passions. And, like all others, he found that after a time insipidity and lassitude was the result; as I was riding in his carriage one day, our subject was the pleasure some persons experienced by accumulating things apparently useless, one or two as examples he named; and I instanced the taste of a gentleman, who had given his life's attention to the gathering together all the published editions of Horace and had collected so many as to fill a bookcase, and which were offered for sale to Christie in Pall Mall, at which place I saw them. The Doctor replied to my remark in a tone that told me his feelings and his then frame of mind—"I *envy*" said he, "him who can find a subject to interest him after forty". Alas! poor man, he was a stranger to the good he envied the possessor. He was born in 1775 and that conversation was when he was forty-two or forty-three years old, he published a work entitled *The art of prolonging human life* but he was not advantaged by it, he died in 1827 aged fifty-two years and was buried at St. Pancras New Church, it being the parish in which he lived and died. A marble memorial to his memory is placed near to the altar, and the tablet eulogises him!

We were but well settled in our new house, when an appalling scene presented itself. I awoke from my sleep, and saw pieces of burning wood flying past the window. Unable at first to speak, I pushed my brother and awakened him; and, it is hardly credible but it is the truth, we did not arise quickly, but first settled the order in which we would arouse the inmates. We agreed that Miss Burnaby should be the last, because as yet, we had not seen her room. I ran down to call my parents; their bedroom door was open. I went in and saw my dear mother but she could not speak to me, being actually in deep suffering. I went down and found everyone had been long up and the danger at an end. The conflagration was considerable, several houses in the street were burned down. I reported to those below that my mother was laughing—they were more wise, instant attention was given and my youngest brother was soon presented to us, who was named John Denton Bagster. My mother's name was Mary Denton.

As the awful riots continued, I was very soon sent to St. Pancras to be out of the way of these direful incendiary burnings. Well, well indeed, I remember my uncle and all the family, after dark, going up to the roof of the house and their counting the fires then burning. I think, but speak hesitatingly, nine were counted. It is foreign to my present purpose to narrate the whole or many of the particulars of these dismal riots, they may be read in the pages of history; I confine myself to what my eye beheld, or, which immediately concerns myself or my family.

Amongst the fires of that terrific night when, with pale faces and desponding hearts, we gazed on the dismal scene from the roof, was the King's Bench prison, which is selected from the rest because of some circumstances most interesting to us as the sequel will show.

Two soldiers of a Scottish regiment were placed as sentinels at the entrance gate, when the mob attacked it. One of them, a man named McQuin, who had been employed as a porter in my father's business and had enlisted into the army—a fine man clear six feet—and was esteemed for the propriety of his conduct in his duties. The mob that came to the prison was numerous and mischievous—they assailed the two sentinels who patiently bare the loud insults and long held their ground, but when the mob threw stones and brickbats, Mac's companion (he was called Mac when in our service) shouted out, "The first man I can mark throwing at us I will certainly shoot". A young man of the name of Allen, threw a brickbat with force and the soldier distinctly observing him throw it, rushed onward to shoot him close that he only might suffer. Allen ran off, the soldier pursued and when the culprit reached his father's dairy yard (which was at some distance from the prison) he entered the cow house and crouched down. The soldier entered and shot him dead. Allen was called a martyr to the protestant cause and was buried with great parade, attended by a prodigious concourse of people, from his house at "Stone's End", to Newington Church Yard, where an elegant monument was raised to his memory by public subscription; and there it now is telling lies in the face of the sun.

Public rumour charged McQuin with the death of Allen, but as he delivered his musket unfired, it *proved* the death was not by his hand. The popular voice however showed itself in wild enthusiasm, for £500 was offered by a committee of the people for his capture. The rage against Mac was a frenzy; in his fright, he fled to my father's house, entering after dark at the workman's door at the rear of the house; and my father being satisfied with his former moral conduct and believing his statement of the occurrence to be true, secreted him until the boiling passions of the multitude had cooled and the law had resumed its legitimate power. This soon took place, Mac then surrendered, took his trial and was acquitted of the charge.

After the riots came the awful time of retributive justice. Many persons were tried and condemned and executed. I went to Mr. Bridge's house in the Strand, to see some pass, who were to suffer death in Gt. Russell Street, at the end of Bow Street, because there their outrages took place. The cart contained two or three men (I think two only) and a lad; he looked boyish and slender. He sat between two men and I was too far off to see very distinctly. Before I left the house to return home, the statement was made that they were hanged and that the boy's light weight prevented the dislocation of the neck and that the executioner sprang on his shoulders to thus shorten his sufferings; but the narrators charged it as an act of atrocious cruelty—but I altogether doubt the fact. Although very many boys and lads were active in mischief, their sentence was generally a short imprisonment and a whipping, and this one boy was the only one that suffered death. The cause of this severity thus arose: a number of witnesses agreed in stating his very extraordinary feats in the work of destruction, even beyond his years. One witness at his trial swore so emphatically to his identity and that he saw him active at several conflagrations, that one of the counsel crossquestioned the witness severely, as supposing by his positive testimony he had some base motive. The witness seemed baffled for a moment by the perseverence and the ingenuity of the examiner. "Though I am sure," the witness said, "I will give it up if a bit of his coat, which I cut off when he was busy in the destruction of property, does not match the place." He then produced the bit he cut off and it fitted. This undoubted evidence sealed the boy's doom.

About the year 1783, though not then understanding the matter correctly, I remember a degree of agitation. I remember the pointed exclamation, one to another. Well! at last America is independent of England. Rich and poor, every rank in society felt this as of national importance, a cause of bitterness and bloodshedding ended.

In this year or perhaps rather earlier Mrs. (or more properly Miss) Burgess, who occupied apartments granted to her in Somerset House, was required to remove from thence (and all others thus privileged) to adapt that building for Government offices, and she removed to us. She was the daughter of Mr. Daniel Burgess, who died abroad while in the service of the Royal Family, on which account she had a pension and apartments in Somerset House. This Mr. Burgess was the son of the Rev. Daniel Burgess, whose traditionary memory still is fresh. This eccentric but good man preached for twenty years in Bridges Street. At the close of that period of his ministry, high "church and king" principles were so rampant and virulent, as to show bitter hostility against the dissenters and the chapel was destroyed by a mob.

He continued his ministry at New Court Cary Street, and it may be noticed as singular that in the time of his successor the Rev. Thomas Bradbury that building was destroyed by the Sacheverel mob—it was afterwards restored at the expense of the government.

Mr. Daniel Burgess and Mr. Thomas Bradbury were alike in brilliancy of wit and vivacity of style, but the former had more solidity of judgment; of him it was said by Matthew Henry, who preached his funeral sermon, that to be of advantage to his hearers he took more pains to be plain than others took to be fine. Although praised by so great and good a man as Matthew Henry, it must be admitted that he sometimes went beyond the discreet use of wit and plainness, of which take a reported instance. His subject the fall of Peter and his denial of Christ Mark XIV.v.71. "But he began to curse and to swear, saying, I know not the man of whom ye speak." Mr. Burgess remarked, if Peter had been speaking in our time and in our language he would have said, "God damn me I do not know him." This was justly deemed irreverent and unbecoming a preacher. It attracted public notice and the dissenting ministers in consequence held a meeting, at which it was resolved, that his intimate friend Dr. Eli Bates and two other ministers of high name, should visit and remonstrate with him. Dr. Bates was renowned for the elegance of his composition and delivery with a sweet euphony of voice—he gained the name of "silver-tongued Bates", and of whom Bp. Burnet says he was the politest writer amongst the nonconformists. He was therefore truly a qualified person to undertake the office, for to him such plain (not to call it coarse and

61

unbecoming) language must have given him pain. The deputation met, and called on Mr. Burgess, told their errand, Mr. Burgess listened to their several admonitions, brotherly and well intentioned, sitting with his head leaning on his hands, silent, at a loss for a suitable answer in justification. He was thus perplexed and had not replied, when the servant came in and said, "Sir, there is at the door an aged woman desiring to see you." "Tell her I am particularly engaged." "I have, Sir, already told her so and she says she will not go without seeing you." Mr. Burgess impatiently went out to the visitor: "Well, what is it you want? But be quick for I am much engaged." "O Sir! Pardon me! But I could not help coming to tell you that I heard your sermon on Peter's denying Christ and you remarked he perhaps said, 'God damn me I do not know him', and, Sir, I said the same twenty years ago and have ever since carried a heavy burden on my heart, and now Sir, I am happy, for if Peter found mercy so may I . . ." The narrative states he almost pulled her into the room where the three Divines were seated and from her lips they heard the matter repeated. Then Mr. Burgess said, "My dear good woman, give me your name," and she did so, and then drew from a drawer a long roll and added her name—then turning to his three friends presenting the roll, he said, "If either of you will shew me a fuller roll, I will try to adopt your mode of preaching." They all joined in saying they wished him God's blessing on his ministry and withdrew, abundantly pleased and wondering.

Great would be my satisfaction could I call to remembrance from whence I obtained the anecdote as then I might, if this channel were accessible have the benefit of securing perfect accuracy in the relation; this is necessary it being above two score years since I heard or read the anecdote. I have given a faithful record of mind's memorial.

Although every biographical dictionary contains the following specimen of his preaching, yet some of my readers may not have had the advantage of reading them and those who have will forgive its repetition. The instance the authors give of Mr. Burgess' quaint and familiar oratory is in his sermon on the robe of righteousness. Says he, "if you want a cheap suit, go to Monmouth Street, if you want one for life, go to Chancery; but, if you want one that will last for ever you must go to Jesus Christ."

My father possessed Mr. Daniel Burgess' dedication of himself to God, written, as was said, with his own blood; a practice not uncommon at that period. Mrs. Burgess, before spoken of, gave it to my father, and he to me. It perished at the destruction of my premises by fire March 2nd, 1822. Some years previously I engraved a facsimile of it which may be seen in M. Henry's miscellaneous works, 1808. A modern writer of celebrity remarks of him: "Mr. Burgess had a wonderful creative imagination and carried it into his ministrations, sometimes with effect; some, who came to mock went home to pray." But at other times it was found better adapted to amusement than edification. Mr. Burgess was born 1645 and died in 1713. His grand-daughter, Mrs. Burgess, died about 1784 in our house and was reputed to be about 90 years of age.

My father was of a disposition to cherish friendship, warm and steadfast in his attachment, zealous in the service of his friends. I was directed by my father to go every Monday morning to the Navy office in Somerset Place to ascertain whether Tom Hardy (as we then familiarly spoke of him) was made a Lieutenant; and I lived to see him bedecked with medals, with the title of Baronet, an Admiral, Governor of Greenwich Hospital and the laudation of the nation. I have lived to see his marble bust in the private apartments of our monarch in Windsor Castle and to hear of a granite pillar to be raised on the Dorset coast to his honour and as a beacon and stimulus to the Navy. At the battle of Trafalgar, in which Lord Nelson received his death wound, Captain Hardy commanded the fleet after the wound until the death of His Lordship and even longer, for the event was not speedily announced lest it should discourage the men in the bloody conflict. On a visit Sir Thomas paid me subsequently to the battle, I asked him if, while the slaughter was so great and death so frequent around him, he felt his mind always firm and unaffected with the scenes. His reply is memorable: "I certainly was unmoved except at one moment when my sympathy overcame my resolution." A deep sigh escaped him: "Good Dr. Scott was shot as he stood by my side and cast into the sea and in falling his body was caught by the tackle of the ship and his bowels were torn out! Oh, it excited deep emotions to see that excellent man in that state."

My memory does not fix the date when widow Holmes on her death bed committed her orphan son, Isaac to my father's care, making my father her executor and trustee. Two memorable incidents belong to this trust. The infamy of a tenant and the reckless expenditure of Isaac, when he attained his majority and obtained his property—the property he derived from his father was not considerable; it chiefly consisted of four houses in Coppice Row, Clerkenwell—Spa Fields then only partially covered with buildings. Two of the four houses were empty and tenants were not easily procured. At length a tenant made application with fair promises and he took possession of one of them, my father entrusting him with the key of the door of the other house to shew any applicants. At the end of two quarters, rent was due and unpaid, the tenant made plausible excuses and said if my father would let him have the other house, which was larger, it would benefit him and the smaller house was more likely to find a tenant. My father gave credit to the statement and into the larger house he entered as tenant. On failure of payment in the next quarter, my father became impatient and said he must be paid. Soon after, he received a letter from the rogue that he had given up the tenancy and thrown the keys into the Thames. The locks were picked and new keys made, when it was discovered the staircases of the upper part of both houses had been used for firewood. The houses were sold for the best prices he could get and the amount put into the funds.

When his ward came of age he received his fortune, the stock being transferred into his own name; but, foolish improvident man, he disregarded all counsel: with the money in his pocket went to Paris and profligately spent his money there, his whole patrimony and he returned to England almost penniless. The condition into which he had fallen occasioned years of struggling for subsistence and at length he went to sea as captain's clerk, behaved well and was admitted as a purser in the Navy and had the charge of the stores at St. John's Newfoundland. Here he lived so many years that I had nearly forgotten him, but, to my surprise he appeared and received a welcome, and after narrating his eventful changes since we met he asked my acceptance of a walking stick, being the backbone of a shark. He continued his visits and in one of them informed me he was daily expecting an advance of rank, and begged the loan of five pounds until the next time his pay was due; but, repayment never came, the shark came no more to my house.

But it is time after this long digression that I return to my narrative. After leaving Northampton school in or about the year 1783 my father gave me the delight of visiting Lyme; and, perhaps, few persons ever painted an expected pleasure in more vivid colouring than I did in the prospect of this visit. The eve of my departure was tedious, I wanted to go to sleep early to dream of the joy I was about to realise.

The Exeter coach left at four in the morning, and as the custom then was, a porter came to the house at half past three to awaken the booked passengers; when he called soon after four to carry the luggage to the coach which stopped at the top of the street in the Strand on its way to Piccadilly. Anxious that all should be perfectly ready in the morning, I placed before I got into bed, all my clothing ready for use and a sum of money for the journey (never before had I received so much) which, when my father gave it to me, he informed me of the proper gratuities to the waiters, guard and coachmen. I placed the money in a broad flat brass candlestick, feeling confident that it could not be overlooked, as the rays of candlelight would fall on it when it was lighted, having to arise before daylight. Hetty came to me before the porter had sounded his awakening noise, she did not light my candle, but left that which she brought with her, and so I overlooked my money and departed without it— it was left in the brass candlestick. The exact time when I discovered my loss and my penniless condition I remember not, but, I know I was travelling some miles before I had an opportunity to speak to the guard about it. Doleful was my train of feelings supposing I should be forced to pass the journey of thirty-six hours without food and should arrive at the end of my journey with as empty a stomach as was my pocket. When the coach stopped for the passengers to breakfast I told the guard my pitiful state. He replied: "I *well* know your father, be quite easy, take your meals with the others, I will clear you all the way down, for though I go no further than Salisbury you shall find it to be as comfortable the rest of the way." What a relief was this assurance! After a tedious dragging journey I arrived at the beautiful village of Charmouth, about one-and-a-half miles north from Lyme. I alighted with my box; not finding my grandfather there, as I was led to expect by my father's prearrangement, I would not go in to the public house but stood by the door with my box, my face directed westward watching for my parent's parent. A short time only I had to wait in suspense—I saw an aged person approaching; I was right in concluding it was my grandfather. In person he was not tall, but upright and commanding, of quick and firm step, his breast bare to the weather, his waistcoat and shirt both open, and I learnt afterwards that so it was in winter as well as summer. I went forward to meet him and saw I was right for his face brightened and without saying, "Who are you?" shook me kindly by the hand and soon were we on our way to Lyme Regis. This town lies in a hollow open to the south, between Portland Isle headland and Exmouth, being nearly equally distant. As we progressed down the mountainous declivity, the prospect of the wide sea on which the sun shone in noontide splendour, filled me with rapture. As however we continued to descend the hill by circumvallation, to soften the descent, the sea was hid and then again its broad expanse appeared to our view, till reaching its own level, we found ourselves in the famous town of my family's long residence.

On my arrival my aunt Edwards gave me a warm reception and not a little did it add to my satisfaction to find that my cousin Ann Bagster was there on a visit.

She was about my own age and a happy companion. We used to go prawning and shrimping together. These fishes are not taken on this rocky coast in the manner they are taken on the Kentish and Sussex coast by the fisher, with a wide net walking in shallow waters at the ebbing of the tide pushing the net before them, but the method of Lyme and its neighbourhood was, to go into the pools and little lakes which were formed by the wear of waves in the rocky stratum of the shore, the stronger veins of the stone preventing the water from receding when the tide ebbs. In these pools we waded and caught shrimps and prawns in a small hand net, and crying out "Oh!" and laughing when a little crab gave a nip to our feet, they were more numerous than prawns. The proud Lyme folk despise the Kent and Sussex shrimps and call them "mere sand bugs" a corruption I presume of the word for shrimps caught on sand banks. A high measure of happiness my companion and I thus enjoyed; we left our shoes and stockings on the beach and twaddled through these shallow pools, not reckoning our happiness by the numbers we caught, as sometimes only a few shrimps and one or two prawns rewarded our toil. One day we considered we had obtained a high prize; we found a large lump of some transparent jelly-like substance, which by tying together our handkerchiefs, we contrived to carry home, swinging it between us. As soon as we arrived we loudly called for aunt Edwards, who, on seeing what we brought with so much labour, indignantly threw it into the river which flowed opposite the house in which we resided, only saying "Why cheelds, what did you bring that nasty thing home for?"

This good active aunt, who was of an ordinary size, came into this world unusually small, her mother's wedding ring was passed over her foot and ankle and the little infant was put into and covered down in a quart mug.

> One of the Lillyputian race
> With bright black eyes and pretty face.

She was an interesting woman, intelligently gifted and exercising occasionally a little poetic talent—as family joy or sorrow called it forth—The monody she wrote on the death of my cousin Elizabeth Bagster, sister to the cousin then with me, who died at eighteen years of age has been often copied at the request of her family; and I regret that a copy is not in my possession to accompany this little tribute to her praise.

This visit to the birth town of my ancestors and the residence of my grandfather, I found replete with abounding happiness during the whole of my visit; it has left impressions which tell of a state of society that has for ever ended and at that very period was in the course of departure.

The situation of Lyme lying out from the great Western Metropolitan road to the Landsend, caused that town later to retain manners and use language that had in general society passed away. To leave on record a few memoranda may save them from total oblivion.

One custom was on candlemas eve, to receive from the chandler a present of what was called "The great candle" (simply what we now call an eight). The chandler gave a "great candle" to every family who saved and had delivered to him the wood ashes they made.—The wood ashes being most useful to him as containing the alkali used in the manufacture of soap. The domestic custom of saving ashes was yet kept up, for my aunt was attached to such observances, and it was on Candlemas eve the "great candle" was lighted up. It was not to be lighted until quite dark, when we all sat around at a table, on which were placed in a broad dish, toasts of bread, *well spiced:* with hot strong beer, well sweetened with sugar poured over them; nor, though the toasts and the beer were consumed no one felt himself allowed to go to bed until the "great candle" was consumed.

The vocabulary and the language too of that and other retired spots of Dorsetshire and Devonshire were different to the general prevalence. Raisins were called fig-ges, two syllables sounded—our figs called dough fig-ges. The plural of nouns was made by adding the old Saxon "en" instead of the modern "s" as housen, postern, etc., and this was general with the Lyme natives. They preserved the genuine mode. We it is, who have changed, only retaining it in the word oxen.

A well remembered occasion of the use of provincial speech presents itself to my pen. My good grandfather was one morning very unwell. My aunt who after her mother's death was very tender and attentive to her father, that morning was keeping the house quiet and I came downstairs buoyant, jumping down on each stair. My aunt called out, "Do ye stalkie, cheeld". Not understanding her, I continued jumping, and aunt in sorrowful anger screamed out, "*Do* ye, *do* ye stalkie,* cheeld." I not comprehending her meaning continued my jumping until I came to the bottom and then I asked her what she said but her anger was much raised at my supposed want of feeling towards my grandfather and want of respect to her voice, which was quite unintentional on my part. To stalk is to tread lightly, noiselessly. The term is now still used in the Highlands in the entrapping of deer and is called deer-stalking, i.e., catching them softly, stealthily.

Another feature of that town and its detachment, from the great trunk of commercial communication, was

* *Note:* "Stalkie" was evidently the old English word for step lightly, and the Scottish term "Deer stalking" may be derived from the same root. E.B.

evinced by the fact that Capt. Domet, who, commanding a trading vessel of Lyme with London, was accustomed to call on his voyages to London to carry letters and execute commissions; and he became the bearer of many messages to and from relatives and friends in the metropolis and his return was the occasion of a lively movement in the town.

Captain Richard Trew, Captain Simon Lee, Captains Samuel and Henry Cox, Mr. Warren and my father left Lyme nearly at the same period and in their future lives were successful: respect and intimacy continued until death but with Captain Richard Trew a close friendship existed, he so loved my father, that when very ill of the dropsy, he hired a glass-coach* to carry him to my father's expecting to die and hoping to die in sight of the house if he did not find my father at home, his desire was gratified in again seeing my father, who accompanied him home, where the friendly captain soon died. He left £200 3 per cent. to my sister.

Captain Simon Lee, above named, after realising wealth retired to Lyme. The only Inn at that time in the town was the "Old George", situated in the narrow street, called Coombe Street, which though curious from its antiquity and holding a degree of fame as the head-quarters of the Duke of Monmouth, yet was not in repair and was more suited to the time of packhorses as chief carriers than the present time and habits of the community. Captain Lee having land adjoining the high street, built an inn and called it, "The Golden Lion". Captain Lee being a capital burgess of the corporation and the "Golden Lion" the best inn in the town, the annual festival on the visit of the Recorder of the borough was there held. On that occasion, the Recorder, the Earl of Westmoreland,

---

* *Note:* By glass-coach was then meant a close carriage lent to hire with two horses.

had directed Grouse and black game to be sent from Scotland to grace the feast: unhappily the cook of the "Golden Lion", spoiled this costly game in roasting it, and Lord Westmoreland with hauteur vowed; with aristocratic asperity declared he would enter that inn no more; and the inn decayed from that time and the feasts were held at another inn until the Parliamentary Reform Bill changed the entire system of electioneering and feasts were no longer known.

Much attention has been drawn to Lyme. The science of geology has had great accession from the coast. Mary Anning of that town has become celebrated for her success in procuring ante-diluvian relics from the lias of this coast, east of the town; the splendid specimens of organic remains, wondrously large and perfect; her industry and ability supplied the beautiful specimens in the Paris as well as our own British Museum, and, on a visit to Lyme years after, I saw a fossil animal about 15 feet long purchased by the Duke of Buckingham for £130.

The discovery of these fossil remains is at the expense of the loss of the most verdant velvet walk my feet ever trod. The grass of this cliff, unequalled for its even close growth and soft texture. The ample walk I refer to was most attractive, being above 100 feet in height and of a good width and seats were placed at suitable distances, it was a promenade few towns can boast; it is gone, nothing remains but a broken mass of soil, forming a heterogeneous jumbling of materials irregularly sloping to the ocean.

The influence of strong south-westerly winds has made great inroads and has approached so near the churchyard and church, that though my uncle Mr. James Bagster had erected a tomb over his daughter Elizabeth before named, intending his own interment there, he so much disapproved of giving his body to the fishes, that he chose to be buried at Hammersmith where he resided at his death.

A sea wall to protect the church itself is really required and the good folks of Lyme admit the existing danger to that edifice, but they do not act. There exist already several sea walls which are kept effective by the Corporation, they consist of a line of massive rocks from the shore to the sea, they slope to a point thus ⎯⎯⎯▷ and as the destroying wind blows from S.W. the wall mightily checks and breaks the force of the waves. These powerful S.W. storms made the necessity of forming a harbour in this bay. The force of the waves when the wind blows strong from this quarter will appear by the fact that I have stood when a child on this wall of strong masonry called the Cob with the sea breaking over as an arch, only wetting by a few drops. The wall slopes on the side exposed to the sea which does not check its effects but rather guides it without resistance to produce such an effect.

Amusement was found by me to stand on this harbour wall when livestock was shipped, for we being at war with France, the isles of Guernsey and Jersey were supplied from Lyme, being the nearest port to these islands and convenient for the supply of Devonshire cattle. These cattle were driven along the wall and the craft was moored close to the wall seaward and then these large animals had a belt swathed round their body having a loop at the back to which a hook was inserted; the crane then raised them and the animals were let down into the transport full fifty feet below. The varieties of the struggles, constituted the attractions of juveniles, for, indeed, not infrequently an ox would make a complete summersault (or Somerset) as Hudibras has it.

> "Some which do the summer-sault
> And o'er the bar, as tumblers, vault."

More than once I have fished for eels from this wall. The manner was, to put a hook into a piece of flesh or any garbage, and being tied firmly to a rope, it was thrown into the sea; but once only was I successful and then I caught a conger eel, so large that I had not strength to pull it up, assistance was at hand and it was secured. While at Lyme my leg was accidentally scalded and my good aunt Edwards, who was a "Doctress of fame" applied with diligence her "never-failing remedy for a scald however grievous" and I was pathetically ordered to be quiet but my cousin Ann proposed shrimping and off were we for a few hours dabbling in the salt water which effected a cure in less time than by my skilful aunt's remedy.

As we entered the house one day my aunt happened to be at the door looking out for us and I having observed a horse shoe nailed on the threshold, enquired "What is it for, Aunt?" She looked at me (her looks expressed wonder that I was not acquainted with its important value) and gravely told me, it was a security against bewitchment. I pertly expressed my entire misbelief; she then said, "and I will give you proof of the power of witchcraft," quickly left me and going into a sort of beer-cellar in an adjoining lean-to, and from an upper shelf she took down a dirty rusty old oblong fish kettle, and confidently putting it before me, said, "into that very vessel, did xxxx (I forget the name) vomit up a great quantity of crooked pins." "Do aunt," said I, "shew me a few of the pins." She took up the tin vessel in displeasure, replaced the treasured curiosity and the conversation ended. Had I not been an unbeliever I should probably had a full and enlarged account of other persons who have suffered by wizards and witches, who she believed dwelt in the black art of divination and blasting.

My aunt had a herbary of domestic remedies, and as

a herbalist professed to cure schrophulous disorders and the king's evil and was not without trusting patients. Her mode of cure was by powders formed of plants, dried by the fire or sun, brought to a fine powder by being rubbed between the hands but she dear credulous woman, embraced too the wide-spread opinion that the hand of the king would cure that malady. Lyme and Dorset and the adjoining county had even stronger faith for they had "in days gone by" deemed the Duke of Monmouth to have so much of king in him; that when he took one of his progresses through the west of England, he was assailed by persons thus afflicted and the cases of cure alleged to be wrought by him were adduced and admitted, as conclusive evidence, that he was not a natural son, but, that his mother was actually married to the king, and he therefore (and being a sound protestant) had a clearer right to the throne than had the Duke of York, he being a rank papist! A curious account is given of this practice in a folio tract published in 1686 which states, "His Grace, the Duke of Monmouth, was much honoured in his progress in the West of England, in an account of a most extraordinary cure of the king's evil given in a letter from Crookhorn (now spelled Crewkerne). We whose names are underwritten do certify the truth of a miraculous cure of a girl of this town, about twenty years of age, by name Elizabeth Parret, from King's Evil. On her right hand, four running wounds, and, two in her arms, also between her arm pit and breast, a bunch which the doctors said "fed the several wounds". Her mother not being able to send her to London to be touched by the King, she had sent her ten or eleven miles to be touched by the seventh son of a seventh son, but of no use!! In this girl's great extremity, GOD, the great physician, directed her to go and touch the Duke of Monmouth. She went first to Sir John Sydenham's, to whom the Duke was on a visit and succeeded to touch his hand, *but his glove was on and a cloth was over her sores* and *therefore* deemed this touch of no value, but she was *sure*, if she touched his bare skin, she would be cured.

On a sudden, to her joy, the news was spread of the Duke of Monmouth coming on; which she, to be prepared, rent off her glove that was clung to the sores in such haste that broke the glove and brought away not only the sores but also the skin: the Duke arrived and the Duke's glove (as providence would have it) hung down (the upper part) so that his wrist was bare; she prest on and caught him by the bare hand-wrist with her running hand saying, "GOD bless your greatness!" and the Duke answered "GOD bless you".

The girl was transported with joy and cried, "Oh, mother, I shall be well."

In four or five days the pamphlet states, all were dried up and the girl was to good health restored. Henry Clark, parish minister of Crockhorn, Captain James Bale, Captain James Sherlock and five others, attested to this truth. This occurred in 1680.

When my time of recreation had run on so that more than one half of the allotted period had expired, I left my dear grandfather's house, my aunt and my companion Ann, with sorrow and it would have been with unmingled regret, had not the image of pleasure to come painted the new scenes with felicitous features.

My next visit was to Chard twelve miles from Lyme, to my aunt, the wife of Mr. Rob Bailey, a dealer in timber to a considerable extent of business. He was of an ardent temperament, in vigorous health and no degree of labour seemed to weary him.

Mr. William Tucker (my dear daughter in law's great

grandfather) met me, as I entered the town. As far as memory serves, he was rather above the middle height, his gait stiff, steps measured and his general mien constrained, as though he had neglected placability, until he had by habit become formal, in other words, he partook of the air of a man requiring deference to be paid to his opinion, because such had been his long experience. His salutation to me is not likely to escape my remembrance either in its tone or its bearing. Looking at me, he said, "I see lad thou hast saucer buttons to thy coat". To feel the force of Mr. Tucker's remark it should be told, that the button trade of Birmingham might be encouraged it was made illegal to use moulds covered with the cloth of the coat, a practice much increasing. To completely preserve the trade was however found impossible and there came into use a new oval button, having a metal rim, white or yellow, enclosing a centre of the cloth of the coat.

I had these sort of metal buttons on my coat, which being new in the country elicited Mr. Tucker's remark. I believe this criticism, so established of him in its tone and manner, that I do not remember having again any interview with him.

Mr. Tucker was a man of the highest worth and of ripe intellect, the author of "Predestination calmly considered". He was neither unfriendly nor uncourteous but his sententious salutation did not harmonise with my sprouting spirit, which at Lyme had been without restraint indulged in pursuit of that which would divert and please.

My uncle Mr. Bailey made the thin winding and pressing boards used by the manufacturers of broad cloth. Mr. Brown, a very superior manufacturer purchased them of my uncle. Mr. Brown lived some mile or two from Chard and once or twice I had the pleasure to carry them for him, for Mr. Brown was amiable and gave me welcome. On one occasion the Rev. Samuel Rowles, who then resided in Chard, and the husband of Charlotte Weston, accompanied me in the walk and pleasant company was he, though sedate he was cheerful and stooped to meet my youthful manners and calling me his "young namesake", with winning familiarity.

As we walked and talked, we saw in the midst of the path a full grown viper basking in the sun, his or her speckled scales reflecting the rays. Mr. Rowles, un-attracted by its beauty, like all other human beings, felt an antipathy to this animal, and, judging by the violence of the attack, his antipathy must be vehement. Though I do not remember whether the onslaught was destruction or not, I do well remember he broke his stick in the attack, nor is it to be forgotten, the pathetic terms of woe in which the good man lamented the breaking of his staff. I was told *what* it was, *where* it came from, how long he had had it for his companion, the journeys he had travelled with it, the danger in which he was of losing it. With a sigh, looking at the fracture "I shall not love a new friend so well".

I will here recreate myself and the reader by the recital of a circumstance which my good father now and then related, that he, when a boy strolling through Lyme churchyard, turning over one stone after another, to see what sort of insects found shelter beneath them, turned up one which concealed a female viper, with many young ones, the size of a knitting needle. The mother viper made a hissing noise, *projecting* her tongue from her broad head, which had the threefold effect, of expressing fear, threaten-ing the intruder and calling the young to shelter, for, while my father looked on, the whole of the young ran down her throat for safety to an inward receptacle, and it is said, the maternal instinct is so strong, that if the danger continues, the mother refuses to let out her young, and they, for want of air, or some other cause, make their way out from her body. Poets give such a malignant character to the viper that it has become proverbial. Watt's verse harmonises herewith which my father generally with pathos quotes when describing the incident:

> . . . as young vipers do
> Eat their own mother's bowels through.

R. Jonson alluded to this dire necessity of the young in the same condemning terms as Watts:

> "Out, Viper! thou that eat'st thy parents, hence!
> Right that such speckled creatures, as thyself,
> Should be eschew'd and shunn'd."

The subject of the viper shall be dismissed with this remark—Mr. Rowles succeeded in raising my sympathy for his stick, but neither he nor I felt or expressed any pity or sympathy for the suffering viper.

Every house was open to me among my relations and friends, and I was truly happy: my super super joy was to go to a farm house near the town, to help suckle the calves, which was done by putting my hand into the warm food provided for them, consisting of skimmed milk with fine meal therein. I put my finger up and the calf thereby sucked up all the food.

There is a crystal stream of pure water flows through this town and there is thus a peculiarity, that it can be directed either into the Bristol or the British Channel, Chard being the highest land between the seas. But in closing my agreeable visit to Chard, the reader must allow me to make a digression, or, rather retrogression, to tell a school incident. He has been already told that I was of frail constitution but he may join me in wondering at a curious remedy that had been recommended by a London physician, which was in the spring at early morn (or other time if then inconvenient) to swallow live frogs; under that advice I did when at Northampton go to the stone troughs on the racecourse for the horses and cattle to drink, there the frogs were numerous. I used to take the little active animals, of the true yellow colour, the real British species, by the hind leg, wash them in the water and swallow them, and I do not remember ever noticing that a gulp or gurgle was excited, for the nimble ones manifested no unwillingness to descend to their cemetery. Brande informs us in his most comprehensive and useful work, that the skeleton of a frog shews no ribs. As to eating frogs, it was the caunting satire of Englishmen, to say of the French, "They are a people eating frogs and wearing wooden shoes". Such foolish epithets have long since died away.

The year 1785 witnessed the great improvement, by the employment of the mail coaches for the conveyance of letters on Mr. Palmer's plan and one of the brightest spectacles of the time was, the annual display of the whole on the King's (Geo. III) birthday June 4th, when the beautiful horses, clean coaches, shining harness, scarlet attire of coachmen, guards and outriders, was put on new. This display evidenced a state of free inter-communication and of mercantile activity that heightened the effect by its glowing associations.

Before the improved mode of carrying the mails was used, the practice was to have letter boxes at various parts but of an evening for the convenience of the public and the benefit of the postman, he walked over his portions of delivery and returned ringing a bell. Individuals paid 11d. each letter but many paid a quarterly sum.

My father paid quarterly and the postman's bell influenced the domestic events of the evening. We had the same postman for very many years, a steady, faithful man; much to his satisfaction he had obtained a like situation for his son. In a sad hour of temptation this son fell, he brake open a letter and abstracted a country bank note. Kemp, the father, influenced my kind parent to try to save his son from death, the laws were then sanguinary and at that time mercy was not influential with the sovereign. The younger Kemp had, before his appointment, worked for Mr. Job Heath, of Fore Street, who willingly joined my father in raising £50 to defend the poor youth. Mr. Erskine was engaged to attend the trial at Kingston. The stolen note was a country banker's note, payable to bearer. The clerk of the bankers swore to the identity of it. Mr. Erskine enquired how he could swear so confidently to *that* note when so many similar had passed through his hands. The clerk said, "I have seen it often—I am certain of it." Mr. Erskine appealed to the judge: "The clerk has sworn that the note has been issued more than once and it bears a stamp suitable for only one issue. I therefore consider the indictment cannot be supported, the note is valueless." The judge concurred and the prisoner was liberated.

My good father having a connection by trade with the best families in the West of England, being frank in manners and of liberal hospitality, he often had the juniors of several of these families at his table at their outset of life and one or two often wholly staying with him. Mr. B. afterwards Lord W. was a very frequent visitor. His conversation was most agreeable, of a rich order, a lively imagination, of ready speech and musical voice. He got deep into my father's debt and saying despondingly to him, that this debt and others overpowered him, my father in reply said, as to his debt to be at perfect ease and added if a loan of £100 would be useful that sum also was at his service, which he accepted to his great relief. Up to that period, notwithstanding his undoubted brilliancy of parts, he was literally a "briefless barister", a brief was given to him and under great perplexity from dread of appearing the first time in court, it is stated, and I believe the statement to be truth, that he went to Mr. Alexander, the eminent special pleader, under whom he had received his legal tuition and training and said, "I am ruined, I am going to leave the practice of the Law." Mr. A. answered, "Why B, are you mad? What is the matter?" "I have got a brief which I will resign, for I cannot plead." "Pooh! I make a proposal to you—I will forthwith give you £500, provided you pay me £500 per year, to begin when your clear income by your profession is £5,000, and not before." He took the £500 and report states that Mr. Alexander received the annuity from the Lord Chief Justice agreeably to the proposal.

It was in this septennial division of my life's calendar, that my parents sent me and my younger brother William, to a celebrated day school at Islington. On Saturday we came home and returned to school on Monday morning, during the week resided and boarded with Mrs. Jones, who lived in Church Row near to the school, the widow of Mr. Jones who lost his life by the fatigue of riding to Northampton to visit his son, as is recorded in the preceding pages. The time we spent at that academy did not exceed six months. I do not recollect whether it took place before or after the visit to my grandfather at Lyme but it took place in the period which intervened between my education at Northampton and going under Dr. Morgan Jones's tuition at Hammersmith, for nearly three years.

The day school at Islington was kept by a widowed lady,

who employed Mr. Gow, famed for his talent in bringing boys forward in classical learning; herein his whole merit centred—allowed any and every freedom out of school, therein rigid and absolute. The school consisted of upwards of 100 boys, not less I think than 120, and like all day schools where the scholars did in groups pass to and fro from their homes free from oversight, many were coarse and profane. The common crime of using the word "damn" as an emphasis in conversation or a superlative in censure or praise, was so common, that my ears had become familiar to its frequency, even in Mr. Gow's presence was it spoken unrebuked. On one occasion in a pet I was thus guilty. The moment the word was uttered my conscience claimed its power. I felt the force of its reproof and was dismayed in my spirit to a degree that would probably not have been the case, had not the moral training of early life and Mr. Ryland's school enlarged the power of this indwelling faculty. Conscience is a man's judgment of moral good or evil, and right teaching carries the decision promptly to a sound resolve, so with me as long as I was at this school my ears disrelished this language, nor did this severe admonition of conscience lose its intensity so long as I was there.

An incident occurred to me early in life, some 60 or 70 years since; I was at Margate with my mother, at which period it was the every day custom of visitors after bathing and breakfast to stroll into the library where, in great variety of useful trifles, toys and bijou articles were spread out to view in glass cases on a circular counter with their respective prices thereon. Visitors would join other listless gapers and joint their 6d. or 2s. 6d. into one sum—the winner was the one who threw the highest number on the dice. I was successful, and a second and a third time. A sad effect was the consequence of this unusual success. I thought, spoke and even dreamed of it, my peace was actually disturbed and when I left the scene and soon after Margate, I resolved never again to play any game of chance and I have kept my resolution. Chess much interests me, it is a trial of skill and not of chance, the most skilful claims the victory—

> The Goddess Fortune let alone,
>   Look not to chance, hold fast your own,
> She is a Goddess always blind,
>   Gives one the kernel—one the rind:
> The truly wise, her boon refuses,
>   For what one gains, the other loses.

At Christmas, 1786, having completed fourteen years I closed my season of instruction and lament that in the later period, the chief period, my tutor possessed not the talent of communicating his instructions acceptably. In this my latter period I do say, without boasting, that my mind was capable of doing more than it did and truth constrains me to say that I was superior to all my class, except one that of the name of Phillips, the son of a tradesman in Gutter Lane, Cheapside, who was *more* above me than I above the others. His superiority was steadily manifested and I ceased to aspire to be first, my emulation became extinct. This talented boy (a year younger than I) went as a clerk to the eminent auctioneer Smith in New Broad Street, ere long became a prominent partner but was by death removed before he had reached the noon of life.

My departure from Dr. Jones's school was signalised by an event which is probably to be found in many others. In this school physical power tyrannised over weaker schoolmates, though in some instances courage in the weaker prevailed over the greater strength in the stronger, as was the case between me and Gwilt who became an eminent surveyor in the City. He was rather younger than I, but stood half a head or more above me and solidly built withal, while I was slim and perhaps under the common standard of strength. The boys urged him on to combat, by using this goading language, "What! Will you let Sam Bagster leave school and you a big fellow not thrash him?" I was placing my garden in order when the boys were playing with him at a running game and induced him to tread on my garden, which raised my threat "to thrash him if he dared to do that again"—he did and after him I went, the boys all saw the fight was coming on. Our usual place for these exercises was in a spacious lofty room once a conservatory to the mansion, when it was occupied by Queen Henrietta as her country residence. We doffed our jackets and tried our ability to hurt each other and, well I remember, my faltering in courage and strength too—even to the low degree of resigning the palm to his prowess, when an accidental catch against my foot caused him to fall and he struck and cut the back of his head against the edge of one of the square brick pillars. Thus ended the fight. As blood flowed freely, it could not be concealed and he was carried to the house with the declaration that it was an accident. My strong opponent did not come out to us all the day and the boys tormentingly twitted me with "Oh! You have killed Gwilt". I believe he is now in full professional practice—I have not heard of his decease.

In this second period of my being, the Rev. Andrew Gifford, D.D. died and my father being one of his executors, the scene of his laying in state in the rooms he had occupied in the British Museum was a matter of exciting interest. His will directed that he should be buried at sunrise but dying in the summer time the executors considered the purpose to be satisfied by burying him before noon. The funeral was memorable—above seventy carriages and a throng of people. The Dr. bequeathed his coins and curiosities of high worth to the British Museum and his valuable collection of the early editions of the Bible to the Baptist College, Bristol. The miniature of the Dr. in my parlour is from the painting in the British Museum and is faithful.

# 1786 - 1793

I left Dr. Jones's school a few weeks before I was fourteen years of age and soon after was placed in the service of Mr. Wm. Otridge, as an apprentice for seven years; he had not a large trade, it chiefly was a dealing in old books and remainders of editions. He lived at No. 134 Strand which house was removed in 1813 to give an approach to Strand Bridge which in 1817 was opened with much pomp and was named Waterloo Bridge in honour of the Duke of Wellington.

The period of my apprenticeship was passed on the whole in an unsatisfactory manner, having to complain of being unemployed than of being overworked. The family consisted of Mr. and Mrs. Otridge, and a son and two daughters. The business persons were Mr. Elias Pullen and Mr. James Otridge, nephew to Mr. Otridge— Mr. Pullen was very short sighted; the focus of his vision being two or three inches. He had lived many years in this service and was esteemed for his moral worth, his general knowledge of books, especially in theology. This near-sightedness was accompanied with a ludicrous manner of shaving, which he daily did below in the kitchen with his face directed to a wooden cuckoo clock, and shaving with him was no common matter for his beard reached to the orbit of his eyes and surely no beard could exceed it in speed of growth and vigour of stem. No capillary filaments I assure the reader, more of the character of bristles and his face was not the only prolific spot—his back had that exuberance of hair that it could be combed. Mr. James Otridge the nephew was of an insipid character, having no feature worthy of note for good or bad; his acts were one continuous series of habitual conformity. Once however he asked me to accompany him, where he would spend the evening pleasantly, and, said he, "I expect you will be interested, some who meet have a very good voice." I consented to go and though the period was fearfully prolific in democratical, if not treasonable assemblings, it did not occur to me that I was about to enter one of the places where such dispositions were cherished. I went merely expecting amusement by vocal music. The room in which the company met was long and narrow, so narrow that the tables were near to the walls, and the backs of the people against whereby everything they received was given over those who filled the seats of the outer side of the table. Before we had been long there the company we found on our entering had increased to about 150 to 180 persons. All seemed to be talking, earnest in their manner. The chairman, who sat at the upper end of the table, soon arose and made a huge noise with his hammer and promptly a pot of porter with a foaming head of froth was placed before him. Another rattle of the hammer brought all on their feet, every eye on him; holding it in his left hand, with his right hand struck off the foaming froth from the head of the porter, at the same time shouting, "So may all xxxxx perish!!" This took place in 1793, the autumn of that year, the King of France having been beheaded a few months before. A thrill of sympathetic approval broke forth, a band of instruments began the then popular french tune ça ira and to which all voices joined, musical and unmusical in one roar. Until the musicians began, who were placed in a small gallery-loft above the chairman, I had not noticed their presence. I felt at once my error in being there and forthwith determined to leave the place, which I did before the ambiguous ardour had completely subsided. As I rose, my determination was made, that I would avoid every notice where I had been in, that I might be able to allege truly, my ignorance of the place of meeting. Until I had reached a more public street than that of the place of unhealthy mental excitement I felt uneasy. Mr. James Otridge continued I think to the end of the meeting. It is due however to him to say, that he only relished the excitement of the scene and the singing. He was of a mild temperament of mind and I believe he was not in the habit of meeting that or any such assembly. He died under 60 years of age, produced by the painful growth of a fungous substance in the socket of his eye, which forced the ball of the eye out and he ended his days in most painful suffering.

I consider it unbecoming to allow my pen to give any personal anecdotes of the family or any narrative of domestic scenes. One amusing change shall be all. We in the business and also the domestic servants were in the habit of using the parlour family language, calling the son Master Jacky; Miss Otridge, Miss Polly; and the youngest Miss Betsey. Much to our amusement and wonder a written order was delivered from headquarters that hereafter, Master Jacky shall be called Mr. John; and Miss Polly shall be called Miss Mary; and Miss Betsy shall be called Miss Eliza. And soon these more suitable names became as familiar as the former trivial names. At this time 1849 I believe all three are living. Many years have run their circuits since I have seen any of the family, the last interview was my meeting with Mr. John Otridge in Bartholomew Lane with his daughter, who by her voice and person reminded me of Miss Eliza as I saw her in my apprenticeship period. Though it is so many years since I saw the Misses Otridge, I depict the two ladies, as demure, respectable persons, occupying themselves with knitting or making ornamental articles for garden pots, etc., or mittens for themselves, active in societies of a benevolent character; who will probably pass from life worn away only by age and then be lamented by their little circle of acquaintances.

The family in my period of apprenticeship kept very little company and of them I will be silent, except of one who not infrequently visited the family and whose visits had features of interest worth reciting and really curious. George Wright, Esq., of Walworth, a gentleman of property, who possessed extraordinary power of amusing company as a ventriloquist, in which he had acquired much fame, not by the usual display of such illusions, as by voices up a chimney or in another voice in reply at a distance nor was it as nightingales or other singing birds, for Paley says, "these birds are ventriloquists for they bring their notes from their bosoms" but by his extraordinary imitations of animals as of two cats "singing love ditties" and now and then interrupted and intermingled by the clatter of two fighting for the priority or two dogs sparring growling and then a right down battle and a grand chorus of these sundry harmonies together would be the finish; and then forthwith Mr. Wright would come into the room wiping his head and face (betokening the strong effort that had been required) and received the full applause of the assembled friends. This gentleman's features were not renowned for beauty but when he meddled with courting or fighting of domestic quadrupeds his face it is said became unnatural, transformed as it were into a canine or feline countenance. Mr. Wright was well aware of the contortions of his visage while thus acting and therefore outside the door exercised his talent. He had a favourite street trick; would overtake a female, and, as he passed, make a noise as though he or the lady had trodden on a cat or dog, and generally obtained his expected reward, a little scream from the female thus assailed.

The room in which I slept at Mr. Otridge's was at the back of the house, towards the Savoy barracks; and, that I may redeem my character as a lover of music (if perchance this may do so) which has been questioned from the time I dropped to sleep at an Orotorio, in the pause between the acts: I bespeak the reader's candid opinion, here me—As a great enjoyment I hastened to bed before 10 o'clock that I might hear the military music play "Go to bed Tom" and by the serenade to drop into sweet slumber—it was a delightful melody, the distance was right to produce a delicate euphony of sound.

In my early apprentice days my good father allowed me sixpence per week for pocket money. He paid me in advance when I left home, with a due measure of paternal advice to keep the half-guinea unbroken as long as possible. This being the first gold that was my own, I carefully placed it in my watch pocket. When, sad to relate, the garment needing a button or some repair, to the shop it went, I forgetting the gold in the fob: in less than an hour my forgetfulness occurred to my mind, and I hastened to the shop and asked for the garment but the coin had been found and he who had appropriated it to himself remained concealed. This was my first pecuniary loss; it affected my spirits for a time. I concealed my loss, being often punished when my fingers travelled to the bottom of the pocket as "through empty space". This loss made my next payment of allowance unusually welcome.

By no means is it my intention to enter business anecdotes in these pages I will confine myself to a single personal incident which the recital may amuse. When customers send for books, not in our stock, these are to be called from other booksellers, and usually, young hands have that to do. On my first engagement in this part of my duties, I called on Mr. Henry Gardner and entered his shop with a diffidence akin to fear. He lived in the Strand opposite to the church of St. Clements, whose charming bells cause passengers to stop (as myself many times) and enjoy their music. They, eight times in the twenty-four hours play Handel's beautiful solemn air (Portugal and two others) which he named Hanover and which name it now bears. Should any of my readers not have heard the mellifluous sound of these bells, I hope they will not remain, to this simple melody, a long stranger, but enjoy its soft swelling sweetness the first opportunity that presents, if not by these bells by the organ or the pianoforte. When my business carried me into Mr. Gardner's shop the street was very narrow and obstructed, but one pleasure was increased by the nearness of the church and the houses, an accession of effect was produced by a multiplied echo discernible when the street is quiet. The houses were built of floor overhanging floor, chiefly wood and plaster, in the ancient style of the smaller city houses and Mr. Gardner was a fit inhabitant of such a dwelling—the shop low, long and dark. The owner kept at the further end, and when I entered, beckoned me to him, and I began to read over the list of books I had to collect. The queer quaint old man gave no reply, but in a tone, which harmonised with his dress (a loose frock coat of russet brown without a collar which he wore the whole years of my apprenticeship) his bearing and his shop. "Young gentleman! Let me tell you, that muffled cats catch no mice. Put off your gloves when you collect books! Meekly did I put my gloves into my pocket and then received the answer, "I have not one of the books that you want."

Changes of dress occur at all times and the one I am

about to notice would probably have remained in oblivion had not a conversation with my father in or about the year 1787 put it on memory. Buckles were commonly used by all persons, for the knees and the feet and to complain of a corn on the instep of the foot was not infrequent. I had two pairs for my shoes and three sorts for my knees, one to glitter by candlelight. At this time a great inroad was made on the trade of buckle-making by the substitution of strings. The shoe buckles gave way first. I went home wearing shoe strings; my father opened the door, he looked and was displeased at my shoe strings, and said, "Do not let me see these dangling strings any more. Do not come over the threshold of my door with these *things* on your shoes." Within two years from that time, I saw my father not buckled but with stringed feet and knees. Such the inroads that fashion on long practice and strong prejudice.

One slight departure from the reverence, the habitual reverence I felt towards my father; the first and only departure from absolute obedience to his will without uttering a single syllable of opposition, arose thus: I was walking up Beaufort Buildings, he was giving me cautions and reproofs. At something he said I was nettled and, bursting into tears, said angrily, "Why Father, no one finds fault with me but *you*!" "Sam! Sam!" was his reply (which I can never forget) "because no one else cares anything about you." I think this took place about my fourteenth or fifteenth year.

As my septennial apprenticeship reminiscences are of a desultory character I mean not to attempt to do more than merely give them as they arise in the mind without observing any chronological arrangement, contenting myself to the bounds of the period between my fourteenth and twenty-first years.

*1788:* In December, 1788, continued into January, 1789, there was a long and severe frost, the Thames being frozen below as well as above London Bridge. I and my brothers went to see a sort of fair held on the frozen surface—it was held opposite the Customs House, etc.

The reflux of the tide did not allow the ice to be fixt to the shore; the broad surface of the ice rose and fell with the tide and left a small open water between the body of the ice and the shore and active poor men obtained a profit by charging a halfpenny for the use of planks laid from the shore on to the ice. The scene has I believe been pictorially preserved by an artist of the day but *I* need none, the scene is in fresh colours now in my mind. Numerous tents and junketings exhibited in many fantastic characters, one pre-lofty, a giant made of snow. There were many booths and stands selling oysters, and as many persons frying sausages and some sold toasted chestnuts and the cry from many voices "a roasted potato and salt for a penny". There was a printing press— the words were composed and on the press, "I printed this with my own hands on the river Thames on December, 1788". The printer asked the name, which he composed and put under, and then the applicant pulled down the press and received his slip of paper to place amongst his curiosities. I believe he was well remunerated for his enterprise and ingenuity. I was there at the breaking up of the frost. The frozen broad surface had two or three inches of water rather suddenly. I hastened to the shore dreading a rush of persons on the increase of the thaw. On coming to the shore not one of the plank owners would allow me to pass without paying sixpence, which I did, leaving a mass of wranglers exclaiming against extortion. Perhaps I anticipated more danger than there really was. However, I was glad to be able to get to the top of the bridge, and others like me had crowded up to see the hurly burly of the removal of tents and stalls and press, and a wondrous mass of matter and of people who had thronged the ice field. Not one life was sacrificed, though one stall with some persons on it were successful in getting on the starlings, notwithstanding the piled up masses of rough ice. Well it was they did so, for the block of ice on which they stood was borne by the flowing tide to the bridge and was pushed up, forming a shelving surface on which they could not hold their position safely. They were by ropes drawn up to the bridge. I saw preparations made but did not wait to see it executed.

These starlings at old London Bridge lessened the water way so much that the water had not room to pass through the arches of the bridge so fast as the tide ebbed or flowed and consequently the gathered bulk caused a considerable fall occasioning much danger if a boat attempted to pass at any other time than when the current had nearly ceased, the water above and below the bridge being nearly on a level.

Many years conjectures and opinions differed as to whether on the removal of these starlings the tide would not flow in so strongly as to flood the low-lying lands on the shore above the bridge and others were of the opinion that it would run out and leave the river with so little water as to be unnavigable except at high or full water but all the varied apprehensions have proved to be baseless.

As it is not likely every one of my readers has read what Pennant, the metropolitan historian, says of this ancient bridge, so different from modern science, that I will give a short abstract:

The birth year of old London Bridge was 1212 and as the present bridge was not completed until 1831 the said old bridge was about 619 years old. The great Charter of the Realm is actually three years its junior. The latter great work shews no decay, the stream of time has not weakened its foundation, and I hope will be in firm existence when the new granite bridge shall by decay and wear require a successor.

Now to Mr. Pennant's description of its erection: "The old bridge was raised on enormous piles, driven as closely as possible together: on their tops were laid long planks ten inches thick, strongly bolted, and on them was placed the basis of the pier, the lowermost stones of which were bedded in pitch, to prevent the water from damaging the work. Round all were the piles which are called the starlings, designed for the preservation of the foundation piles." Esto Perpetua!

About the year 1789 a change began in the cut of the hair and the use of powder, which arose from an approval of the practice of the French, who adopted cropped locks as a symbol of revolutionary approval and the destruction of the horrid bastille had moved the mass of the English community to sympathise and imitate the French example, but this practice was less followed when the faithlessness of the first consul Buonoparte and his rancour against this country appeared in the virulent atrocity and wicked tyranny of detaining English traders and travellers in France and putting them into prison. Amongst those he detained I knew several—Mr. Payne the bookseller in the Strand and Captain Willson, the husband of my brother's wife's sister who, with a host of others were confined in the fortress of Verdun. Captain Willson escaped from confinement by hiring a dealer in crockery ware to carry him to the Dutch seashore and thus did Captain Willson escape from his imprisonment: he lay on straw beneath trays or rows of the ware suspended over him. At night he was relieved by a walk by the side of the cart and reached his home. Few, however, thus reached British ground, for such the malevolence of the tyrant that he would not allow an exchange of prisoners and the number at Dartmoor and in hulks were very numerous, a great burden on our finances.

Before this hair cropping became the practice Mr. Duncan proposed a tax on perfumery and Mr. Pitt glad to have an article to tax, signified to Mr. Duncan his desire to reward him for his suggestion. Mr. Duncan was a baptist minister in Wales with ten children and his fixed income forty pounds a year.

The vain man made the extraordinary request that he might have the honour of Doctor of Divinity and forthwith from one of our Northern Colleges came the dignity of D.D. His title of honour was at the expense of his common sense.

In 1787 I was a spectator of Lunardi's ascent in his balloon, which had long previously been on show at the Pantheon, Oxford Street. The aerial journey, or rather voyage, began from the Artillery ground, near to the city road. I was on the roof of a house in Bunhill row looking on to the ground. It was a thrilling sight; I was in some slight danger for in its ascent it struck the ridge of an adjoining house but received nor occasioned other damage. This first ascension of a balloon in this country caused a wide and deep sensation through the whole community.

Two years after, in the year 1789 it was, the Bastille of Paris was destroyed by the mob, which has been before noticed. The populace of London became excited to a degree that partook of frenzy—I say frenzy, it was so strange a mixture of republican ferocity by the rabble, with a quixotic real joy by the higher classes to see a great nation delivered from despotism of government and the levelling to the ground of a prison in which the prisoner had no power to obtain his trial or permitted to have intercourse with any one. Apprehensions were felt by the reflecting, that a popular outbreak would take place in London, as the mind of the community was so feverish but loyalty and peace, though they were assailed, happily prevailed.

In this memorable year it was that George III went in grand procession to the cathedral of St. Paul's to return thanks to Almighty God for his recovery to health and reason. His visit called forth such exuberant national exultation and loyalty, that neither before nor since have I witnessed the like. The people even in courts and alleys lighted candles from attics to cellars. St. James's Square had large wax flambeaus on every other rail. Mr. Hope's house in Cavendish Square, said to have thirty lighters, was not all alight at 2 o'clock in the morning. The joyful queen came to see the illuminations in a private carriage and was detained by the blockage of carriages five hours, till three in the morning. The whole population were in the streets the entire of that memorable night.

Cowper has written some pretty lines on this warm display of national gratitude, to which I refer the reader— they will please him.

Very amusing and surprising are the nostrums which, at different times in my short span, have obtained notoriety, each ten years seems to have its own panacea. About 1789 the all-cure value of tar water was loudly trumpeted, a sure remedy for diversified ills of the human nature, except poverty and old age. Its merit was widely admitted by the intelligent portion of the community. The promulgator of its high merit, from personal experience was that close thinking scholar Dr. Berkley, Bishop of Cloyne. Mr. Otridge was a warm advocate for the use of it. About once a fortnight while the whimsy existed in fragrant approval, we had a new brewing, and my task it was to be the brewer, which was thoroughly to mingle the best Norway tar with the approved quantity of water and occasionally to repeat those stirrings for two or three days, and then it was fit for use. On one occasion I was despatched to Mr. Fuller, the banker in Lombard Street, with two bottles of this tar water. It was a sultry afternoon and upon my presenting these fair twins of aqua vito, the banker said, "take them upstairs". I did so and in a minute up came Mr. Fuller. I had put down the two bottles and was wiping my wet forehead. He threw a sixpence into my hat and said, "Give my compliments to Mr. Otridge" and downstairs he went. Mortified was I at having a gift that was such a reduction of their banking funds!

Mr. Otridge was also a professor of the practice of influence on the system, became a patroniser of the metallic tractors and found some wise (?) persons to receive the benefit of his skill.

A very painful display of popular error I saw at this time, and reflection on it deepens my conviction of their misjudgment, yet the principle of their conduct was self-preservation: the public had strangely adopted the opinion that the extensive buildings, named Albion Mills, at the foot of Blackfriars bridge, on the Surrey side, were erected to monopolise wheat and flour, to accumulate the store corn, and thereby control the flour market and thereby make the price of bread higher. Then it was almost at a famine price which gave the destructive impulse to the multitude. This spacious substantial pile of buildings took fire, it is alleged by the friction of the machinery in grinding, but whether so or by an incendiary is yet a mystery. When I arrived the people were in a frenzy of joy at the conflagration. Their maledictory earnestness became active to prevent the firemen from using the engines and that strong built spacious concern perished, at a loss to the proprietors of £25,000.

In the year 1792 my highly esteemed tutor the Revd. John Ryland died at Enfield. His memory is and ever will be fragrant.

In the period of my septennial commercial pupilage, it was part of my care to give out and receive back the books which were sold with coloured plates, and they were three: Hill's *Vegetable System* twenty-six vols. folio, Edmondson's *Heraldry* two vols. folio, and Evelyn's *Sylva*, two vols. 4d.

The colourer, whose name was Langham, was poor but truly honest; his poverty had not warped his integrity. Occasionally he was closely pressed for means, and I, sometimes, granted a payment in advance and I did so more frequently and readily because he acted faithfully. His wife was of a mild disposition, very active in helping him in his business, sending from home with clean linen and dividing his scanty supply with apparent content.

Years after this period, I heard of the affliction of this worthy woman. She suffered under the malady called polypus, which had its root in her nose and required removal of its branches by pincers, an operation most painful to her and disagreeable to a surgeon. I recommended her to the sympathy of my friend Chevalier (whose portrait by Hayter graces my parlour mantle) an eminent surgeon, who, for a length of time periodically attended her. After much suffering this, and other complaints, brought her near to death, and when dying she told her husband, "I have in all our troubles saved one memorial of my once prosperous condition. You will find a china basin on the upper shelf of the cupboard. I beg and enjoin you to deliver it to Mr. Bagster, with my heartfelt thanks for his kindness." The basin I have preserved as a memorial of this kind woman's character.

Sir John Hill, was a bustling busy body in literature, a miscellaneous multifarious writer; beside the *Vegetable System* in twenty-six vols. Folio, he wrote a herbal of sanative qualities and some farces for the theatre. He was always in some turmoil, wanted to become a member of the Royal Society and was blackballed. He was stung to the quick and wrote a sarcastic work entitled *A History of the Royal Society*, wherein is exhibited the way to breed maggots and the question discussed if boiled fleas on boiling, would become red. With the Reviewers; with the Royal Society he was continually contending. *The History of the Royal Society* consists of extracts of the philosophical transactions which are feeble and admit of joke and insult. The Society left the work unnoticed but Garrick, for the players, gave a brilliant retort:

> "For physic and farces his rival there scarce is,
> His farces are physic—his physic a farce is."

My pen refuses entirely to overlook the last named work coloured by poor Langham, because the diary of the author John Evelyn, Esq., has been published within a few years and gives so much interesting information of the occurrences of his time, that it is one of the most readable and amusing books with which I am acquainted. He died about 1708.

Mr. Edmundson, the author of the *Body of Heraldry* above named, was a herald-painter of eminence, but much it is to be regretted, he died in impoverished circumstances, his son sold all his stock of heraldic books to discharge his debts, but his mind and firmness gave way and he attempted to drown himself in the great ponds to the south of Lord Mansfield's mansion. He failed to accomplish his purpose, in consequence of the deformity of his person due to a broken back in his infancy—he floated, struggled to the bank. His determination of suicide was not checked—he went to the gate of the field, leaned on it and cut his throat and continued in that awful position until the event was discovered.

During my apprenticeship, in consequence of illness, I went to Lymington in Hampshire under the medical care of Mr. Greathead ("nomen omen") whose claim to the honour his hatter can avouch—his hat was made from a block of extra size.

The town of Lymington is at the head of a tidal river, which flows up to a bridge of raised causeway. Above the bridge, the water in a mere rivulet but seaward, having its estuary to the sea near to the Needles (rocks so called), when the tide is at flood it is very wide. A short distance from the town there are salt works. The flatness of the land on the shore and its water from the sea flowing calmly in, gives a power to receive the water or to bank it out, by this peculiarity these salt works have been established and carried on. The salt water is admitted into broad reservoirs about eighteen inches deep and then excluded for several tides, until evaporation has carried off much of the water; it is then allowed to pass into a more shallow reservoir and thus from one to another until the salt has parted with so much water that it will bear an egg on its surface, when it is pumped into a vat in which heat is applied and crystallation follows. Its quality is similar to Epsom salts, but chemistry has discovered some combinations that can produce the article at less cost and the manufactory languishes or is wholly neglected and forsaken.

When the river was filling by the tide flowing in so gently that the surface was as smooth as a pond, I hired a

punt to poke about by myself, but, being unacquainted
with the peculiarities of that river, which, on the ebb tide
empties itself with great rapidity, I was left suddenly on
the wide flat of mud, far from the shore. The mud I
ascertained to be too deep to venture on it, but how deep
I knew not. My paddle was pushed in so deep as to shew
me my danger—being the afternoon, the next flow of the
tide would be dark. I became terrified and was about to
use my lungs to best effect, in hope to be heard, when at a
distance I heard a voice but saw no one, "Do you want
mud patterns?" This was music to my ears, and "Yes"!
was loudly shouted. Soon a man came walking on the mud
with patterns for my use. They are flat pieces of wood
fastened to the foot by straps, and glad was I to tread on
terra firma. I visited Yarmouth in the Isle of Wight, and
was amused, by the crier of the little town with a paper in
his hand and a large bell. He stopped before the inn; I
opened the window to hear his notice:

"Please to take notice, that Thomas xxxxx will to-
morrow kill a fine ox and he requests the inhabitants will
this evening let him know what part they wish to have
that they may not be disappointed." I suppose that town
is now so large that several oxen are weekly necessary for
the supply.

The town of Lymington is almost on the borders of the
New Forest and not far from Holdre-bride, the residence
or near to it, of the Rev. Mr. Gilpin, vicar of Boldre, with
Lymington. Mr. Gilpin was a most useful and elegant
writer—to him we are indebted for the introduction of
the delineation of picturesque beauty in the narratives of
his several tours in parts of England and Scotland. A
taste, by his pen and pencil, was awakened to relish
scenes of beauty in a landscape, which prior to his work
had been nearly neglected. Kip's bird's-eye views and

Grosses' castles and antiquities; elevations naked and unadorned, with the formal views of gentlemen's seats in country splendour, with gardens cut into squares and a moat around, took a different field from that we call "picturesque"; a word familiar to our ears, which owes its birth to Mr. Gilpin—a word correctly used when describing the combination or groups or attitude of objects appropriate for the painter. The perusal of Gilpin's pages is useful, to this day, 1849, as I ride through the park, I trace his points of beauty in the union of two trees or in the grouping of several and I have even thought his taste had guided the planting of that dense mass of verdure about a furlong before the descent towards Virginia Bridge. Though desultory in style, the perusal cannot fail to add such a love of the beauties of nature that is abiding and useful. Mr. Gilpin was soon followed by Mr. Repton, a private gentleman, who attained to celebrity in ornamental gardening and adopted it as a profession and is said to have obtained £500 for laying out the verdant part of Russell Square. While the houses were in progress of erection, I ascended to one of the upper rooms to view the arrangement of the shrubs and paths and the effect met my admiration.

The last work I read of Mr. Gilpin (and I believe the last work on his favourite theme) was entitled *Forest Scenery and Picturesque Beauty*, two vols., published in 1791, wherein is a touching narrative of a scene in the New Forest. Had I Mr. Gilpin's pen, I would essay to produce an effect on my reader equal to that which the perusal had on me. I read it with the most thrilling interest; imagination must supply what my pen fails to produce.

A keen sportsman unacquainted with the peculiarities of the place where he was enjoying the pleasure of shooting wild fowl which frequented the broad sand on the retreat of the tide, was on this extensive field of sand, and so eagerly intent on his sport, as not to notice the tide was already returning and had covered the lower ground on the land side of the mound on which he was shooting. To get to land was impossible, for, to his dismay he found the tide had flowed in and completely encompassed him; as he could not swim he determined on the course to pursue. He ascertained the highest spot and there fixing his fowling piece firmly in the sand to enable him to keep his position and prevent the water lifting him off his feet, he stood firm, determined there to wait until the tide turned. He did not know how high it would rise, he had no alternative but to wait the issue. The tide came in very gently, the uncovered sand lessening and reached the spot on which he stood. The water steadily advanced and deepened around him until it reached his mouth—then was he forced to stand tip-toe. In this painful and critical position, rocked with the tide, uncertain after all whether he would persevere and preserve his breath if the water rose but a few inches more, for every small undulation of the water washed over him, he thought he observed a change in the advance and retreat of these undulations and *hoped* they came not so high. He eagerly watched each succeeding undulation—O the transport of his soul!—he saw again the top button of his coat! Such is the summary of an extraordinary deliverance which 58 years since I read with intense interest. I desire to leave Mr. Gilpin in the full sunshine of the reader's favour, by informing him that his publications were successful and profitable and that he appropriated the whole of the profit from them to found a school for the poor of the parish of which he was the rector.

In the latter part of my apprenticeship I did for some

time (but my remembrance of the length I forget) attend a French lady to get instruction in the French language. She resided on the first floor of a confectioners not far from Bedford Street, Strand. She was between forty and fifty years of age, of ready wit and had so good a store of materials for cheerful chat that few English women could equal her.

Business carried me about this time to call on Mr. James Matthews, who lived at No. 18 Strand, a bookseller, who took me aside to ask my advice as to the best manner to be adopted by him to check the taste of his only son, who seemed determined to go on the stage. I thought it a little out of the way, for a grave father to consult me, a mere stripling but answered as wisely as I could, for I had been previously cognisant of his taste and very favourably attracted by his son's peculiar talent for recitation. When young Charles Matthews (for he it was) came into Mr. Otridge's shop, we have induced him to jump on the counter, which he would do with the ease of a gazelle, and recite a speech from Shakespeare or from Beaumont and Fletcher, which he did with pathos and point and not seldom he would end it with a jeu d'esprit of impressive or ludicrous tone or gesture.

Having thus been amused by his son, my mind was not so grave as the father expected, for I felt that he had a special talent to please and would certainly excel. My answer was, "I do not know what to reply to you but I think you cannot check and change him effectively, unless *you* can fill up his whole time pleasingly and profitably." Poor Mr. Mathews got no good, nor could he, by consulting men of mature judgment gain any advantage, for his business was so small as not to afford any real employment for his clever son.

Mr. Mathews' Saturday practice was to go regularly to

Whetstone, to preach at a little meeting house in that village, some eight or nine miles from London, and Charles availed himself of this weekly absence to attend the French teacher I have above introduced to the reader and in her rooms pursue his theatrical taste. The bedroom, in which stood a four-post bedstead, opened into the front room by folding doors and a curtain in the doorway divided the rooms. Charles arranged this bedroom as a stage, the persons sitting in the front room to witness and applaud his vivacious actings. My custom was to go to my own home every Saturday evening, by which I did not once meet the comic lad there but my old friend Mrs. Slatterie did—she took lessons of the same French lady and well knew Charles Mathews.

The elder Mr. Mathews was in person portly, of a florid complexion and his walk was with measured steps, as though he carried thought with him. On one occasion, a clergyman overtook him and fancying him as doing weekly duty in a neighbouring church, asked him to do duty for him the next Sunday. This Mr. Mathews agreed to do and thus a plain tradesman preached instead of their usual preacher: neither the clergyman nor people knew the fact; Mr. Mathews kept his own counsel. I determined once to go to Whetstone to hear him preach and I did so. The meeting house was the smallest I ever entered, the pulpit placed at one end, a sort of table pew, with several music books on the table of it. At it I sat, it held some ten or twelve persons and occupied with the pulpit not much less than half the place the remainder not having above six or eight pews. When the service began the clerk, who sat at the head of this table, his back supported by the pulpit, named the hymn to be sung and read the first verse and as soon or before the last word was well pronounced, I was really appalled, no less than four shrill clarionets brake forth in full wind and so strange an effect did it have in that little place I have not before or since experienced.

An accident I am about to relate, which I am not disposed to deny myself the amusement of circumstantially stating; so much amused was I when it occurred. The quire stock of books at Mr. Otridge's were stored in a spacious lower warehouse at the rear of the dwelling, amongst this mass of books was a considerable number of bundles, containing Bowers' history of the Popes, in seven quarto volumes—a work much sunk in money-value and as much in public opinion, because the author was vacillating in his creed; now protestant now papist was he. The book was seldom sold; a copy was required; I had to bring one from the warehouse and to my surprise and amusement, I found convenient provision for the comfort of young rats. Maternal love and instinct-skill had prepared a comfortable nest by nibbling the Pope's into small morsels and had arranged the papal chips in a true dish-formed circular shape—the snips of paper being evenly spread around. Although the preparation for fecundity was very perfect but there was no other means of ascertaining how many broods had thereby been comforted and reared in this silent security but the quantity of manure *behind*, not a speck in the front, would have called for the bushel basket to carry it to the dung heap had it occurred in the country. Can the question be satisfactorily solved, were the progenies thus reared in the bosom of the papacy, improved or deteriorated in their character thereby? It is as difficult to settle, as to fix the creed of the author; on this point several angry pamphlets have been written and the controversy was hot. Mr. Bower was born of Roman Catholic parents and bred in the faith, he became a protestant, again returned to papacy, and his widow, after his death with much formality, attested he died a protestant.

The birthplace of this papistical brood of rats reminds me of the trite story retained by juveniles in all schools for 200 years past, of the wit and severity of the still famed Dr. Busby, who was fifty-five years headmaster of Westminster School. Dr. Richard Busby was celebrated alike for his unflinching disciplinarism when wielding his academic sceptre as for his abilities as a classical teacher.

In his right hand the birchen rod he held, and with every misdemeanour queld the advance of the youth under his tuition was memorable and notwithstanding the severity the school flourished:

> By him 'twas held as law divine,
> That boys grew wise by discipline,
> Woe he! who missed just concord once,
> The Dr. called him, "Sleepy dunce!
> And need my lad a gentle jogging;"
> By which he meant a wholesome flogging,
> Then by way of demonstration
> Gave the poor boy a flagellation.

Although the stern Dr. as a steersman neglected not the stern part of his duty, he was open hearted and vivacious, encouraging wit and fostering academic progress in the school and favouring the best scholars. The single display of this fact is generally known to boys at this time, few are ignorant of it. It so happened that while the scholars were at morning prayers, a rat descended into the room down the bell rope and the mirth of one was so irresistibly moved, that he burst into loud laughter. As soon as prayers were over, the Dr. angrily enquired the cause of this unreasonable merriment. The wit of the youth spared the Dr. the exercise he had contemplated. The boy replied to the enquiry,

"I could not help laughing
Because a rat for want of stairs
Came down the rope, to say his prayers."

But to return to the rats which so abounded at Mr. Otridge's, their increase can be accounted for Malthusian principles, their food was in abundance. The next house was occupied by a butcher. A curious circumstance in connection with these rats occurred. In the evening of the day the cook had fried some savoury edible for supper, the pan was placed in a corner near the sink—it had not been there two minutes before a rat came from a hole beneath and jumped into the pan but jumped more briskly out; the pan he found too hot; then he put his tail into the fat and then licked it; the hot grease growing cooler, he again got into the pan, and several, not six feet from him, much amused and really laughing aloud but he unabashed entered into the full enjoyment of his hot supper and, seeing him so absorbingly engaged, I reached a small hatchet hanging within the fireplace and killed him in the pan before he had ended his luxurious repast.

Before or after the above event I know not but seeing a rat within the entrance of his hole but his tail was out, I seized it with firmness and thought I had him; he struggled away with a skinless tail—the skin of the tail was my only reward.

More about rats—Mr. Walsh who resided in the Strand a chemist and maker of "Walsh's" Ginger told me that he, being in anticipation of a day's pleasure on the Thames, had to meet his companions at Temple stairs at break of day. Before the time he was there and seated himself on the dwarf wall at the head of the steps, and while thus waiting for the arrival of his friends, was mightily surprised to see "an army of rats" (so he called a long broad line) come down the lane and pass to the river, not one descended the stone steps but as each came to the edge, dropped down to the right and the left, entering into the sewer drain, it there having its outlet to the river.

Now 1849 while writing about this voracious and prolific animal, I will narrate a recent anecdote: Mr. Bourn, the executor of my late friend and neighbour Mr. Kemp Grundy, informed me a few days since, that Mr. Grundy could fascinate rats, partly by an attractive winning manner to animals and more direct by a powder and paste he prepared, which was as agreeable to their olfactory nerves as to their palate. It would be out of place here to the philosophical consideration wherein consists the attractive power of certain odours to rats and cats and all animals, but certainly their respective tastes differ from those pleasing to human beings, as much as one kind of animal does from another. Mr. Bourn stated that the rats were so pleased (both mouth and nose) with this seductive mixture, that they would come up to Mr. Grundy's legs, sit on his knee and eat from his hand. Mr. Bourn added that unless he had heard it from such a man of truth or himself seen it he could not have thought it possible. He wished to see and asked permission of his friend to be once present and Mr. Grundy readily acceded to the request, saying, "but on the condition you keep very quiet, for, to them you are a stranger." They went together to a barn, a place for grain but then empty. They sat down and when thoroughly quiet Mr. Grundy whistled softly—after a while a rat appeared, then came one after another. He scattered some of the bewitching composition near him, which they ate greedily. Then he threw some on his legs and knees, more came close and soon he had 13 or 14 around him, some on his legs, some on his knee, feeding from his hands. Afterwards he scattered poison mixed with the pleasing mixture and was freed from them for several years. Mr. Grundy was offered (Mr. Bourn stated) £100 for the secret but having pledged his word to the communicator not to reveal it he kept his word and the secret is lost by his death.

Perhaps I have dwelt too diffusively on the rat subject; I will conclude it by setting common opinion right on the origin of the brown rat, so destructive and so widely spread —it did not come from Norway but from Asia. The British "black rat" has become nearly annihilated by the intruder from Asia. The "black rat" is smaller, of more graveful mien and form, having a finer fur and much less ferocious.

The French Revolution commenced its career and made progress during my apprenticeship and when the bastille of Paris was stormed and destroyed by the populace, the sensation (already before noticed) convulsed the multitude in this country. England throughout was in a transport of enthusiasm, one feature was a crowd attending Debating Societies which increased in number. The character of them was intensity of feeling, infidelity and rank republicanism were with zealous energy held forth as the panacea of all evils. The excitement became too vehement and extensive for the government easily to restrain the feverish mass from outbreaking to open rebellion. No less than six stringent acts of Parliament were needful to curb the turbulence of the multitudes that assembled to lead the nation from their loyalty to the throne: the largest gathering took place in the Copenhagen Fields about a mile to the east of St. Pancras old church.

The face of society was really changed by the French revolution; altered in *many* respects; the people's manners; their apparel was affected by it. As an apprentice I wore a cocked hat, and powder adorned my head, and from the snowy top a tail descended and tied with silk bow a la ton.

The prettiest exhibition of the head dress of men appears in the portrait of Garrick appended to Davies's life of that great actor. The painter's name does not occur to me. Mr. Garrick died when I was about seven years of age. Hogarth the painter died some years earlier but both their widows have received my courteous bow. Reader! look again at my frizzlings performed at a shop a few doors distant, by Mr. Thomas a man of capital business. I contracted with him to dress my hair three times each week, as many of my neighbours did; there were two classes of customers, those who did not provide their own hair powder and combs and those who did; I was in the latter class and had my japanned dressing case with my name on it, taking its place with others, placed on two shelves, a comely array with their golden inscription of names. Frequently several persons came together, which required patient waiting, but each took his turn in the order of his arrival. On one occasion Mr. Thomas gave a preference and I lost my turn and as my patience was much tried that morning by long waiting, my unpowdered head felt the indignity and in a huff I left the shop and it eventually produced a reason for employing Mr. Bond, a rival ornamenter residing nearly opposite. The change much pleased me, I seldom had to wait and he had an assistant named White, who was a brilliant workman— his touch, his speed, his execution, far superior to my earlier frizeur and when I had completed my apprenticeship and in business, he daily ornamented my head. As I sat one day under his operation, with the morning paper in my hands, brimful of the sanguinary deeds of the Parisians, my eldest brother George, bounced into the room to tell a melancholy event. "Sam! my cook's husband has blown out his brains." "I did not know your cook had a husband." "Nor I, until she told me so less than an hour since." "What is this husband?" "She has only been married a fortnight to him. He is a barber in Old Round Court, she says, he shewed me about thirty guineas a few days since." "What can be done to serve her?" It was agreed the best service he could render as her master and friend to lock all up. We went together and on the ground lay the poor wretched man, his blood flooding the floor, his brains spotting the ceiling and a hole in the window, not scarring it, through which the bullet passed after his death blow received from it.

White was present at the narrative to me and the next day to him I said, when dressing my hair, "Here's a fine opening for you to begin business." I said this because I knew he was courting a young girl living as a servant with Mr. Fairman the book binder in Helmet Court. Said he, "I should like it much but I have not money enough to pay for the fixtures and furniture." I lent him what more was needed and he got into the shop.

The event occurring in my parish, I took proper steps to be on the jury to find out what had become of the thirty guineas he had so lately possessed, which could not be found. There was one suspicious fact, the lodger in the first floor saw him before anyone else and when he saw the catastrophe, returned to his room *before* he called attention to it. This gave reason to suppose he had robbed the body; the money might have been used in the sad practice of gambling in the State Lottery, not by buying or selling shares of tickets, but by betting on the probability of certain numbers being drawn in the first hundred each day—many poor have been ruined and lost their life or reason by such practices. Lotteries are happily now no more a means of supply to the state and much misery is thereby averted. The shop was of the humblest class and below the fair average, there was smoking, gin drinking, vulgarity and indecency, the coarse profligacy of low-minded and conceited political wranglers. White soon changed the face of all things, no longer a foul cloth beneath the chin on which the juices of gin and tobacco had dribbled; now, a clean cloth as clean as the apron he wore. Within the first year his loan was repayed to me. In a moderate time the shop was changed from a mean and disreputable to a respectable and profitable business. His talent was soon discovered, he was a perfect artist in his vocation, and the shop being a corner shop he used one of his windows for the sale of knives, razors, soap and perfumery. The order, cleanliness, ability and frugality found its reward. He saved money and his gradual increase he put into the funds and I believe it exceeded £2,000. He had at the price of £800 bought his own freehold house and here from came his fall. The Commissioners for the improvement of that part, required his house and gave him about £1,100 for it. White thus became the possessor of a large sum and at the same time lost his employment. Money and time were both in his hands and he was puzzled. He carried his upward progress to wealth uninjured, but this sudden sum upset his balance of mind and made him aspire to a higher walk of life than that he had hitherto enjoyed and grasped for gain in a new adventure.

Mr. White entered my shop after a *long* absence, I had almost forgotten him and I was ignorant of his success and of the favourable issue of the sale of his house and business to the Improvement Committee. He said his visit was to ask my *help* (not advice) for that he was going into the bookselling trade! My astonishment was at the highest, I really could not easily give credit to it, it was unhappily true and he was so far committed in his ruinous course, as to have taken a shop in one of the streets diverging from Blackfriars Road, had fitted it up, had bought a Circulating Library of Novels, and he added: "I am studying catalogues (of which he had two with him) to qualify me to purchase at sale auctions." Also he said, "I further want to consult you how to get the Post Office to my shop in this new street." I told him the applicant would be required to find two persons as a security—as sureties— "O," says he, slapping his breeches pocket, "here is my security," a demonstration he was beyond counsel, inflated and purse proud. As he left he said, "I will come and ask your advice again." I did not see him again for a very long season, I think two or three years. He called, was full of bouncing hope, in buoyant spirits and said he had bought an harmonicon for little more than £??. (I forget the sum but it was large) and have obtained good rooms in Cornhill at a fair price, considering it is this public part of the city, and have engaged in a capital musican to play on it for two guineas per week." I asked, "But what is become of your shop?" He replied, "I can buy well but find no customers afterwards. I have given it up at great loss, but to the harmonicon everyone is to pay 1s. to hear it and it plays every instrument that has been invented and in about a month it will be in complete order for exhibition."

Poor White! I saw him no more until penniless, ill shod, beard sprouting, linen and flesh unwashed, a houseless wanderer—I know not his end!

The eventful history of this man evinces that he could steadily hold the cup of increase while increase was gradual, but when the sudden stream poured in he lost the balance of the cup, the wealth ran over and turned his regular habit of action upside down. Of him, my opinion altogether is that from his upward progress to the sad final downward course, he was steadfast in good intentions and sobriety. His memory bears the impress of pity on my mind towards him rather than censure. The effect of sudden accession of wealth on him, was similar to its too well known sad effects on many of those persons who obtained capital prizes in the States Lottery. I know but of one exception, the present Mr. Rusher, Bookseller in Reading, who held half the ticket that produced the £20,000 prize.

In connection with the Debating Societies which were suppressed, when they were perverted to an evil purpose, I will sketch an amusing scene. It took place at Coach-maker's Hall, where Mr. Otridge was occasionally a speaker. The President at the close of each meeting gave notice of the subject for the next week's debate to allow speakers to prepare their minds. Mr. Otridge had a very peculiar and paradoxical way of treating a subject, whereby he was by Dr. Gifford playfully called Mr. Puzzlecause. At these meetings for debate each speaker was allowed twenty minutes and Mr. Otridge was in the marrow of his prepared matter, when the bell tingled. The president addressed him, "Sir, your time is out" and he resumed his seat. The speaker who followed satirically said: "The gentleman who last addressed you Mr. President, all will admit to be a person of talent, he is full of matter, master of the most pleasing property of an orator, to keep the subject in suspense and thereby add to its interest—the proof of his ability will be generally admitted, for no one present, I do not exclude the orator himself, I say no one present can tell which side of the question he supports, nor on which side he will stand when the question is put to the vote—(laughing and jeers). I find by your approbation of the orator that you are solicitous to learn to whom you are indebted for this display of rhetorical ability in the speech just delivered, the speaker is Mr. William Otridge, who has published an elegant volume called *Solitary Walks* by George Wright, Esq., and the author is as clear, clever and agreeable as the orator who is the publisher, for that work contains the sublime poem of *Death and my Lady* and a portraiture of them both!" There are extant several speeches made at the Debating Society held at the Queen's Arms in Newgate Street by the Rev. Augustus Toplady in his collected works vol. 3, edition 1825.

# 1793 - 1800

Having in the preceding pages closed the recital of three
of the periods of my terrestrial existence, Infancy, Boyhood
and Youth, I enter on my Fourth Septennial, my fourth
week of years from the age of twenty-one to twenty-eight—
1793–1800.

> Important Era! Time its course has run,
> While Earth hath three times seven gone round the sun,
> Bringing me onward with it to the stage,
> To use the knowledge gain'd in pupilage,
> To carry into practice, now—as Man,
> Some well arran'd and wise commercial plan.

> Important Era! Whence some facts we trace
> Of public gloom—to *me*, of special grace
> Direct from GOD—a precious gem from Heav'n
> Received in seventeen hundred ninety seven—
> Sweet is my task—to sing of wedded bliss:
> I hail the year, Annus Mirabilis.

My apprenticeship terminated about the time I attained
twenty-one years of age and was concluded with some
dissatisfaction with my master's fulfilment of his duties,
who had never displayed the slightest intention to increase
my knowledge or that of my two fellow apprentices, there
always seemed to be a latent jealousy: Neither was I
satisfied with myself, I felt on retrospection I had not
availed myself of as much as even the limited scope
allowed, neither had I sedulously cultivated my mind as
my leisure afforded opportunity. My future purposes at

that time were not at all fixed, I was somewhat inclined
to go into some other book-seller's employ for an increase
of information, but time however for commencing
business drew nearer than I expected. In 1794 my brother
George went into Mr. Robinson's shop, No. 81 Strand,
where he carried on the trade of a confectioner and pastry
cook, to eat a cake or tart and was told that Mr. Robinson
was about to resign business and leave the house and that
the lease was to be sold. My brother instantly felt the
house would be suitable for me; my father and I were of
the same opinion after looking at it, and approving, we
that evening went to Mr. Dent, who owned the lease and
was the uncle of Mr. Robinson, who carried on business
in Portugal Street and who had a country box at a place
near the New Road called St. John's Palace (why so
called I know not) and bought the lease, my father paying
a guinea to ratify the bargain and as part of the purchase
and well it was that my good father with his usual decision
and energy so did, for the second day after Mr. Dent asked
my father to rescind the bargain. On his negative, he
offered £100 to forgo the contract as he much wanted it
for a particular friend. This offer made us well satisfied,
and proved the purchase of the lease was made on
advantageous terms.

On February 8th, 1794, my father completed the purchase and the lease was conveyed to me and I took
possession. I found the one pair floor was occupied by
two young persons, the Miss Fallowfields and the two
pair back room in the use of a Mr. Wingrove. The former
were dressmakers of some fame and Mr. Wingrove was a
jeweller in the employ of Messrs. Rundell and Bridge.
Mr. Wingrove told me it was his office to attire the Queen
when she wore the crown jewels. He gave me this account
of the robing scene. The robing was at St. James's Palace,

the room had looking-glasses on every side and court etiquette directed that when anyone faced the Queen to bow and that bow being reverberated by the reflexion on every side, he always returned with a bad headache. He was paid three guineas for his attendance.

He shewed me a stomacher and a sprig of ivy for a head dress (worth £10,000) made for the marriage of the Princess of Wales, which took place in 1795. These inmates I found to be very agreeable honourable persons and the house was as quiet as though I lived alone in it. We should I doubt not, have lived together much longer than we did, had not love to a dear object moved me to move them, to make room for my chosen wife.

Before I enter on this pleasant theme I have a few incidents to place on these pages which took place about this time, such as the circumstances which followed my taking possession of the house and some passing scenes of men and manners.

The late tenant's property was all removed, except the iron door fixtures of the oven, to remove this two men came and with a donkey and panniers to carry it away. While these two men were at work, my father and I were in the front kitchen adjoining, conning over matters in reference to the repairs and settlement in business and while thus we were musing and conversing, the two men who were in the adjoining room getting the iron work loose to remove it, fell into rank discourses, their language awfully rebellious, threatening destruction to the government. We heard their bad discourse with surprise and pain. We went to them and my father addressing the principal, who seemed so to be, by his manners towards his companion and by his general bearing. My father said, "How could you allow yourself to utter such language as I have heard you express?" The man left off his work, laid down the tools wherewith he was loosening the iron door from the brick work, and stood erect, assuming a posture that befitted a hero. He stood, a model for a Cornova to sculpture Napoleon holding the sceptre. His manly figure, his brawny legs and arms, nourished by his hard labour—a fine specimen of robust symmetry—his face as black as smoke and soot could cloud it, while his eyes shot new-lit energy from his black brow and skin

> As pointed diamonds being set,
> Casts greater lustre out of jet.

The build of this man harmonised with his impressive mien

> Fine symmetry with limbs of brawn
> A perfect model to be drawn—

He, looking intensely at us with his speaking piercing eyes and treading with one foot a half-step forward, said, "Sir! did you see my donkey at the door?" "Yes, I did." "Sir! (holding up and spreading out one side of a worn jacket, in a manner between us and the light) Can you count the number of holes in my jacket?" My father made no reply. After a short pause the man said pointedly "I ask you *Sir*! Can I be worse off let what change soever happen?"

Would he not have proved a Brutus if our times had been the time of Tarquin's sovereignity? We left the man satisfied with his own conclusions but as soon as we were out of their hearing, my father said: "After what we have heard , not I, nor you, nor anyone that has ought to lose would desire a change."

That my predecessor had not success in business was no marvel, for, when we began to clear the basement, we really found more rotten plum twelfth cakes in a large vault at the rear of the premises and of rotten cranberries than a cart would hold and a single horse draw away. The weight of cakes was computed to be not much less than a ton.

On April 19th the shop was opened. My night was restless—arose early—myself took down the shutters of the broad window, which I had filled the preceding day and, following the example of my late master, the prices were put on the books. The shop had not been open much more than an hour, when Mr. Bastard of the Crescent, Southampton, purchased a set of Johnson's *Poets* 45 vols. and other books to the amount of eighteen pounds. Truly joyful and hopeful were my feelings on this early sale, it was regarded as an omen of future success.

Quickly in the back room I ate my breakfast and got again into the shop, taking care however to replenish the window with other books before I went to my smiling meal. In a few minutes after my return to the shop, my father's dear friend Mr. Wm. Bailey entered. "I want a Family Bible." Soon was he suited but was disappointed in losing the pleasure of being my very first customer—this pleasure he had anticipated and came confident of enjoying it. I wish it had so happened that he had been first and bought the Bible before Mr. Bastard's purchase. This gentleman continued to be a customer until his death.

Having at some length narrated the interview and conversation with the men who removed the oven door it is apposite to be followed by recalling to the readers' remembrance, that the Gallican Revolution had revolutionised the great mass of the people who were ripening for outbreak and rebellion, and to this end clubs of men having evil designs, and talented members of such clubs delivered lectures of great atrocity to inflame the multitude. Their ardent elocution to rouse and give life to malignant passions was widely influential. The soil of the public mind seemed prepared for acts of outrage and crime and, this was scarcely averted by Mr. Pitt's energy, though clothed with the power of six bills of restraint that for that purpose then passed and which obtained, amongst the mobility the name of "gagging bills".

One of the most able and desperate of the oratorical crew was Thelwall who harangued at meetings, held in a spacious room in Beaufort Buildings, Strand, but of this more hereafter.

My residence in the Strand began in 1794 and was continued until 1816 when I removed into our present business premises in Paternoster Row. My immediate neighbour to the west in my Strand house was a widow who had one daughter of rough blunt manners and in the department of dress by no means neat nor was she clean in her person; she had many points in her favour, being sober, industrious and persevering in obtaining orders in her business for the honest support of her aged mother and herself. Her father followed the occupation of dyeing and scouring, etc. Miss Veale was so frank and blunt (almost coarse) that no one fully approved her manners, yet all agreed in considering her honest and well intentioned and felt kindly towards her and her widowed parent. The residents next to the west of Mrs. Veale were Messrs. Code & Adams, they being next neighbours on one side and I the next neighbour on the other side.

Mrs. Veale and her daughter notwithstanding their industry and economy, became so embarrassed that the Landlord had threatened to seize their goods to pay their rent. I pitied them much and went to Mr. Code and suggested to him how great the kindness it would be to relieve the widow and daughter by paying this rent.

Mr. Code agreed therewith and we gave an equal sum and our neighbours obtained relief from that oppressive debt. Miss Veale whose tongue was always equal to her occasions for its use, was now prompted by gratitude loquacious to those many ladies who employed her in praise of this liberality and amongst others to the widow of Mr. Packwood, who for many years obtained public fame and realised wealth by the manufactory of the renowned "Packwood Strops" for sharpening razors. Very unexpectedly the above little act of kindness and benevolence produced an important result. Some years after I had removed from the Strand into Paternoster Row Mr. Code called on me. I was at the end of the shop distant from the door; he entered with a bounce and without closing the door came bustling up to me in a manner I fail to depict. His approach was so peculiar that wonder started up in me—What does this strange frenzied manner indicate? In an instant he had reached me and in a flurried abrupt manner, "Do you remember that you and I paid Mrs. Veale's rent several years ago?" "Yes! I remember it well." Scarcely waiting my short answer, he added, "a lady to whom Miss Veale told the affair has left me £10,000." "Well!" I replied, "I presume your visit is to tell me that I am to have half that sum." "Oh, no, no." "Why it was my invitation to you to do it." "Umph." "You will, I conclude, give me at least a handsome service of plate." "Ha, ha, ha," was his rejoinder and then with nervous almost morbid hilarity he went swiftly away without even a "Good morning!" or grace on departure. He left one thing to do, to shut the shop door after him. Since I have not seen or heard aught of him. The emotions of his extreme joyful surprise were almost caricatured. Mrs. Packwood I suppose having neither relatives or friends, happened on her death bed to remember Mr. Code's name, my name not then presenting itself to her.

Notwithstanding the intentions I have expressed to exclude trade occurrences, I will introduce an incident or two that occur to my memory. As an example, I will state an amusing transaction. An order for books came by the foreign post, a reference with the order removed every scruple as to the safety of the execution of it and it was consequently done. The time had fully expired in which payment was expected. I wrote to my correspondent for the payment. His reply was different to my expectations: "You would long since have been paid but the payment is delayed, solely because I have no medium of money payment but I can send produce," and enclosed was a list of articles he would invoice to me. I chose dried skins of goats. I had no correct idea in what state they would arrive, nor what they would be worth, nor what persons could use them. It was nearly a guess matter when I chose them. In due time their arrival was announced consigned to a merchant on my account, who offered me the tempor-ary use of a warehouse near London Bridge, to which place they were removed and the duty on importation paid. A person applied to me desiring to purchase them, an appointment was made for the applicant to view them, he proceeded to look at and examine them, and, as he pro-ceeded and turned over the skins, I could not discover the principle by which his preference was influenced, he did not seem to take those I deemed the best. "I am willing to buy those (pointing to what he had selected) what is your price?" I replied that I wished to sell the whole to one person. "No," said he, "I will give you so much for those I selected." I said as a sort of half jest, "You meant to double your offer." In fact he did double his offer and I sold them. On this he said, "I will in half an hour bring the money and take them." In half an hour he came with two hackney coaches and when completed and delivered, I asked the ground of his choice in the selection. I was quite at a loss to know what had guided his choice. He stated that he purchased them to use part of the hair to make "Brown Georges", and lest any of my readers should need an explanation, I inform him or them that our aged sovereign, George III, had adopted a snug flaxen wig of the colour of the hair of those chosen goat skins, which wig had become popular and in common intercourse in society was called a "Brown George". When the sale was completed the buyer added, "I like my bargain and would have doubled the price I gave rather than have lost the skins."

There was at this time a tradesman resident on Ludgate Hill named Dalmahoy (of whom remembrance is still preserved by the name being still continued on the shop) who had such a character for good taste in the article he sold, with elegance of dress and polished manners that truly in many respects he led the taste of the town. This very wig was by him invented and first worn, bore the name of a Dalmahoy until it was adopted by the King when in honour of him it received its new name, "Brown George".

My father wore such a wig for many years; in his miniature, which graces my room, he is seen in it.

These goat skins would not now realise so good a price, this wig and all extrinsic ornamental locks are dismissed by the wiser use of nature's best covering—is the language of 1849.

> Though head be bald and shine like glass
> The wig, and powder, not survives
> True taste declares you can't surpass
> The fashion that dame Nature gives.

In what year I am not able to state but I remember carrying some books in a hackney coach into W. Smithfield and passing through Old Bailey at the broad part of the street near to Newgate Street, I saw the embers of a fire on the stones, which were almost extinguished: over these dying embers the wheel of the coach went and as I got out of the coach, I asked the coachman the cause of that fire. He replied: "there has been a woman's body burnt for murdering her husband." Was this information true? I write as I heard and like to be satisfied as to the fact. Revolting scenes of olden days were, such as burning alive and putting traitors' heads on poles at the city gates, as they were at Temple Bar.

The capital punishments of death inflicted for various crimes were at this period awfully frequent, a relic of days of greater cruelty gone by: the benignant and milder exercise of justice at this time causes the mind to recur to that period with horror; every sessions several suffered death. Newgate was in a doleful gloom and the condemned prisoners almost in despair at the awful suspense until the Recorder's report arrived and those doomed to die were named, sometimes as many as ten and twelve perished. I saw from Mr. Birch's window in Holborn, eight persons pass on their way to Tyburn to be hanged; four were in a cart and four were drawn on a sledge, to represent the old mode of dragging culprits on a hurdle.

> So have I seen amidst the grinning throng
> The sledge procession slowly dragg'd along.

The multitude are not slandered when I call them a grinning throng, the most unbecoming levity prevailed. Those on the sledge were guilty of forgery and coining.

To a very different subject my pen shall be employed. This was the period of Pamphlets, the diurnal and other periodical publications not having become influential as it at present is.

Politicians and other writers made their opinions known to the public mind by this means and very respectable shops were chiefly devoted to their sales. The names of these booksellers are remembered and respected: Almon, Debrett, Walter, Stockdale, Wright Ridgway, etc., the whole phalanx are departed and have left no successors. The age of pamphlets has passed.

In 1794 the despotic cruel mode of impressment for men for the naval service, with the abominable tricks in enlisting soldiers, had created such an enraged opposition that crimping houses were destroyed by the infuriated people so that press gangs and crimping were no longer employed as the means of supplying the army or navy.

1795, October 27th. My good grandfather (whom I have introduced to the reader's affection and attention) died at Lyme aged 87 years.

In 1796 a tax was laid on bachelors which continues to this day. Everyone is still required on making his return to the assessors of the taxes, if a bachelor, to attach a B. to his name. I had not long to pay it for a dear beloved object had taken possession of my heart and soon after did of my home, on which pleasing subject I now enter but I will not dismiss the subject of taxation until I have named one against which the general voice was heard in disapprobation. This was a tax on maidservants, which, by the united force of wit, caricature, ribaldry and strong opposition was repealed.

I hereby give public notice, that when I am a member of the Commons house, I will propose, that a heavy tax shall be laid on every man who slights the state of matrimony and that the tax shall not go into the public treasury, but shall be paid to those old maids who have no objection to enter into that holy and happy state!

In this same year the Government appealed to the people for aid to carry on the war on the continent against the French and proposed a loan of eighteen million: to it was given the title of the "Loyalty Loan" and wondrously did the public feeling respond, the whole was subscribed in a single day. In this loan my father took his share. But taxes, loyalty, disloyalty and other themes must now give way to introduce to my dear family (and I write to no others) who read this, the most influential circumstance of my life, my marriage with my precious wife, my loved companion through now fifty-two years of my pilgrimage.

The circumstances which led to the happy result of a life-companion in all respects suitable for me, are these: my parents had long been in warm friendship with Mr. John Birch, his wife and family. Mr. Birch and my father were acquainted before either of them took to themselves wives. They used to meet with some other pious young men of whom we may name Mr. Burford and Mr. Ashlin (to the latter my youngest brother married his daughter) with whom the intimacy existed even until death: they went together at times to hear Mr. Romaine preach on a week-day evening; and it is well here to notice, that it was at Mr. Romaine's lecture, that Mr. Birch first met *his* excellent wife Charlotte Henrietta Johnson Welldon. I was once at this lecture at St. Dunstan's in the west parish church in company with Mr. William Hodder, the eldest son of Mrs. Hodder noticed on p. 15. It was in the year 1793 or 1794 but the service has fled from my memory altogether, except the circumstance, that the church was nearly in darkness, having only candles at the pulpit and desk and it was alleged to be so, because the rector did not approve Mr. Romaine's doctrine and therefore would not allow him to have the church becomingly lighted.

The friendship of birth in their bachelor days continued through life; beside occasional visits, it was a settled rule that once a year, the Bagsters should dine with the Birches and once again the Birches should dine with the Bagsters. These dinner meetings were always on a Sunday because Mr. and Mrs. Birch could not leave their business on a week day, nor could the younger branches of the Bagster family all assemble on any other day. On one of these occasions that we were invited and the day fixed, but my father made a mistake and we went a week earlier than the invitation.

My mother and I were as usual together, we arrived first and quickly observed, or thought we did, that we were not expected, though Miss Eunice Birch was the only one of the family at home, she was not in the least flurried in manner, but received us with the same courtesy as though we had been expected. The dinner was evidently not ready and there seemed no preparation for a large party, so my mother and I said, "We will take a walk if there will be time before dinner." We did so and when we returned found the long table laid in the large front room upstairs and the knives, forks, glasses, etc. in order. Our little friend Miss Eunice was very busy and seeing her stoop to a corner closet which stood in this room to lift out additional plates, I said, "Shall I help you, Miss Birch?" The ease and pleasantness with which she replied assentingly, won my heart and *it* pronounced the decree, "This shall be my wife!" The company consisted of seven Bagsters, Mrs. Morris and the Birch family, in all thirteen persons. The dinner was a small leg of pork boiled and a roasted hare. The whisper went to each Bagster, "Do not eat much, our visit is evidently a vexing mistake."

After all was over the congratulations were general and sincere, that we had, though not expected, fared so well. "How great events from little causes spring."

The flame was not allowed to lie smothered long, and considering it to be a privilege to have discreet parents to consult, I stated to them my wishes and received their entire approbation. Good Friday soon followed, when some of Mr. Birch's family were invited to spend the day with my parents at Pancras, where at that time they resided, having retired from business when my eldest brother George married (which was in 1793) Miss Sarah Sumner (the daughter of Mr. Joseph Sumner) who was a most sweet and interesting woman.

Pancras was at this time a pretty rural village, few suburban villages more attractive, only a house or two were between my father's and King's Cross.

My entrance into love's labyrinth was soon discovered, in returning home from this visit I offered my arm to Miss Birch, and we managed somehow to wander from the rest of the company into the remoter part of a brickfield through which we were passing, and a laugh was raised against us. Mr. Prosser who was paying his addresses to my sister Mary, was one of the party and indulged his vein for fun and merriment at our expense, and even old Hetty said she was sure that Master Samuel was thinking of Miss Birch. The fields we were then passing, are now Russell and Bedford Squares with the several streets adjoining. On the next Sunday I went to Orange Street Chapel, where Mr. Birch's family attended and so it happened, that the dear girl was there alone. I pitched upon her in the midst of the crowd, after the service and offering my arm escorted her safely to her home. Not many days after having heard of the opening of a new chapel by a popular preacher, I asked Miss Birch if she would like to be present: she said she would. I said I should be happy to call for her and accompany her there. On walking home I determined to make my mind known to her, my courage was not equal to the resolve, I was silent on the subject until we had nearly finished our walk. I proposed another perambulation round Bloomsbury Square, during which my wishes were expressed and with sweet simplicity a willing and direct answer "if her parents approved".

"E'en *now*, with thankful glee I oft retrace
The Yes! which crowns that square—the honoured place!
Sweet yes! my heart did *there* its purpose gain!
*That* yes! The brightest link in life's long chain."

Our love declared mutual, the rest of the walk made the mind blythe and hopeful. I took leave of her in the passage and we bade each other a significant lingering Good Night. I went to rest contented and hopeful, with a new train of future circumstantials on my mind. It was found the parents of both were equally willing. When the time drew near, that we were to be married, I gave the information to my servant, who was a clever, tidy, willing woman, but she feared the difference that a young wife would make and to my regret gave me notice that she would leave my service and another was hired but my bachelor servant Mary who dressed with the plainness and neatness of a quaker, continued to reside with me after the marriage and when she left said she much regretted leaving, now she knew the wife I had obtained.

The marriage took place on December 19th, 1797, on which day the King (George III) went to St. Paul's to return public thanks to the Almighty for Lord Duncan's victory over the Dutch fleet off Camperdown in June preceding in which action Lord Duncan took eight sail of the Line.

As the procession passed my residence in the Strand, it was filled with visitors, amongst the rest was Mrs. James Bagster and family. She said in her own blunt usual manner of speech to my friend Mr. Barber, whom I had appointed by locum tenens to offer refeshments to my visitors. "Where is Sam? I dare say he's gone to be married."

Our wedding dinner was comfortably provided at Mr. Birch's and all passed off happily, the elder Miss Percival being bridesmaid accompanied us home.

An annual assembly of the whole of Mr. James Bagster's and our family was held at each home, my turn happened on the Christmas day, only six days after marriage and as I had no room in the house large enough to entertain so many, we dined in the shop availing ourselves of the day closed from business, nineteen sat down to dinner. On reflexion I decidedly consider it would have been well to have deferred the wedding day or have postponed the visit to a later time. This delay then did not present itself as a question, perhaps Mary being yet with me had some influence. Six days after marriage to have such a company had more of the bachelor's vivacity than the married man's discretion. One end was accomplished, the two families in all their branches became at once mutually introduced.

Memory has its pleasurable recollections, cherishes my love to retrace her worth in all the train of events that called it forth. I love even to look back and see her as she was in tender years and girlhood.

> Though so many years are past
> Kind memory holds possession fast.

I brightly remember her while now writing as she looked when taking out the plates from the cupboard and accepted my assistance so naturally and so gracefully. She was remarkably small, the fashion of dress being tight and trim gave to her a further impress to the symmetrical smallness of her figure. "What a little wife Sam has chosen", said my blunt aunt Mrs. James Bagster. I could have told her that the most precious jewels are preserved in small caskets. But my remembrance, if I may so say, was earlier than that, not indeed then as the companion of my life and sharer of my joys and cares, but as a little unconscious infant. In the year 1777 it was my dear mother paid a lying-in visit to Mrs. Birch, and as usual, I was her companion, I then being about five years old. Imagination spread my wings and gaze on the little cherub-looking innocent, and sweet in her cradle with a beauteous cap of skilful needle work and corresponding lace! It is not unreasonable to suppose that she from me received a gentle kiss that her slumber might not be broken. This very dear infant became and is still the object of my sincere love; and, it *is* delectable, step by step to trace the path I have walked lovingly with her until now, having attained the age of 77 and she of seventy-two and of marriage fifty-two years, I do express my heart-felt gratitude for the blessing she has been to me. I close this account of my courtship and wedding by adopting the name of one of Milton's immortal characters as truly appropriate for her—

"The happy mating woman—"

and truly my children's children and all who are privileged to know my amiable active wife will confirm her just title to it.

This year 1797 in which my happiness was promoted by the marital union is most memorable for many other important events,—It is in my life "the Annus mirabilis".

I will state some things in this period connected with public events, shewing it was of general importance, no year of my life more productive of interesting events. It was therein, that the Bank was by order of the privy council authorised to suspend the payment of their notes in gold, and paper to become the circulating medium for one pound and higher sums. This important step, this most adventurous step, was told me early in the morning on which it was to commence. I was almost thrown off my mental equilibrium. On looking at it, reflection drew such a grim picture that I frightened myself with my own gloomy speculations, I loitered and did not go in at my usual time to breakfast. The clock struck nine and having some cheques in the till and one of them receivable at Gosling's bank in Fleet Street, I neglected my breakfast, ran to the place and entered the banking house before business began. I presented the cheque. The usual question was not asked "How will you take it?" I said, "Give me gold." "We do not pay gold today." "Pay me as you please." I had thus received *proof*, that the report was true, that the bank had suspended *cash* payments and that the bank-note was a legal tender in discharge of a debt and the use of gold usurped by paper. There were writers who approved the measure and stated that an enlarged and cheap issue of paper money would add to national prosperity—increase commerce by a larger circulating capital. Others more wise foresaw gold would disappear and such were confronted by noisy assurances that we could get rich without gold and the parliament declared a bank note to be of equal worth to gold. The result of debate and argument may be summed up by saying, nothing but extreme necessity, only to escape from national bankruptcy could justify the measure. The wits and the grumblers were not silent.

Guineas no more passed as 21*s.* but were hoarded or sold to money brokers for exportation to the continent to pay the troops. Silver became nearly as deficient as the gold and as a shift Spanish dollars worth about 4*s.* 6*d.* were issued at 5*s.* having on each the small King's head similar to the hall stamp put on silver plate.

In this memorable year bread was very dear and suffering widely experienced. The supplies for our immense army and navy exhausted home produce and stores. One of these defenders on foreign service consumes more than three persons at home and the provision contracts brought a class of characters as dealers in corn and other commodities and made the market price rise higher than even the natural effects of too large consumption. In 1800 the quartern loaf had risen to 1*s.* 5*d.*, and second or household bread only allowed to be sold. The baker under a penalty of five shillings a loaf, forbidden to sell bread until after it had been baked twenty-four hours and he was forbidden to bake a pudding or a pie, without receiving with it a certificate or written declaration that it was for a sick person. These regulations reduced consumption but produced the effect of raising the price and deteriorating the quality by inferior mixtures and before the year ended the loaf had risen to 1*s.* 10*d.* and partially to 1*s.* 11*d.* which price with some fluctuations continued until 1810 when it again became the price it bore in 1800. This wondrous price continued so long as to change the whole agricultural population; those who held farms on lease rose above the state of mere farmers who became rich by frugality and skill and gradual accumulations; became soon, to their pleasure and surprise opulent, and took the rank and expenditure of a higher class, called "Gentlemen-farmers". The farmers were many who were yearly tenants to whom the landlord raised the rents and as leases expired new leases were reluctantly granted but none on terms agreeing with the lofty prices that grain secured. To this period 1849 the baneful effects have not entirely lost their influence, in as much as farmers have lost in a considerable measure the mien of plodding industry and are not satisfied without great gains; and, at that time the landlords getting rents too high have receded too slowly to regulate the fair relative value between landlord and tenant; whence sprang the stirring conflicts on the Corn Laws. Soon will free trade in corn produce a very different result in obedience to the *lex necessitatis* which the competition of the produce of foreign lands, must prove a severe trial on the landlords and growers of this taxed country. When the quartern loaf was at the very highest price, I went one evening to hear Mr. Thelwall deliver a lecture on Political Economy, and if energy of manner claimed the chief praise, he deserved it. He appeared in my opinion to owe much of his popularity to the intonation of his voice, he gave his long periods a wide range and though involving much variety of expression to be clear, it was kept distinct in its parts and the sentence usually finished in a melodious arrangement of words—his inflection of voice from low to high, from soothing to horrifying, was impressive and effective. Yet, a cool hearer, as I was, amidst an exciting assembly, saw no solid claim to laudation when the audience applauded loudly. His metaphors and illustrations were sometimes becoming an orator, at other times he was too homely and affected the passions of the unreflecting. I offer an idea of his address to his mercurial listeners. He was on the topic of the deplorable effects of the enormous price of bread and all provisions. To this effect he spoke "Distress! Distress! Look into the single room of the artisan in the attic above or cellar beneath and observe the dire features of poverty. See the poor pale faced wife rising from her seat, her broken chair, to visit the plump smooth self-satisfied harpy who takes the garment of the half-clad, half-fed mother in pledge at less than half its value." Then the orator with adopted tones gave the dialogue between the pawnbroker and the wife, depicting the mother as now returning more disconsolate, having received for her deposit of a needful garment not enough once to feed her famished children, who had been left desolate while she was gone on the mournful errand, and, as she returned to her hungry flock provided herself with the morsel of bread which the amount of her pawning produced, and, as on her way home meeting one and another of those unfeeling hard hearted men who daily carry *a roll on their heads* that would be sufficient to feed at least one of the children, pining, nay dying, of hunger. Shame! Shame!! was the outcry, which gave the orator breath and arrangement of his thoughts. "Shame indeed! Did you not deeply feel at the recital of such woe, if you would not be men and if you do not condemn and execrate our rulers who have brought our country into this state you would not deserve the name of Englishmen!" (Applause—widening sensation). He continued after a pause. "Some may ask where is the husband of this Englishman, where the father of these destitute innocents, dwindled and shrunk by want? He is a wanderer through the streets, seeking employment and not finding it is doomed to starve or to enter into the army or navy for bread leaving his wife and offspring to the tender hearts of the sympathising merciful parochial overseers. In every sentence he courted applause by closing with a sort of euphony of tone. His rhetoric was enriched by paraphrasis or variety of demonstration, which his lively imagination, vivacity of manner, action and command of language enabled him successfully to use. His elocution deserved praise. I considered however, that he had more of glitter than the solid and substantial thinker and close reasoner. My calm meditation was interrupted by the consideration whether his *able* peroration by which he so adroitly concentrates the pathos of his argument into his concluding words produce an effect on his cropped hair audience that may induce a personal insult to me, who (to use his words) had a child's roll on my head, in plain language, my *hair was powdered*. I looked around to see how many persons were thus guilty of starving a child and I saw only three others who were robbers of the food of starving infants! I occasionally counted the four, soon I saw one depart and then another—I, then, after sitting a few minutes that my snowy head might pass without notice, I quitted the company. The only danger, if any, was at the bustle when the lecture was over, for there was but one door to the place. This incidental reference to white polls fixed the evening in my memory which otherwise would have escaped as much more important have done. Thelwall had a poetic talent, the following is a specimen:

*Stanzas on Happiness*
Who is the man that's truly blest?
    Not he who in inglorious ease
Saunters through life;—whose sordid breast
    The sensual joy alone can please.

Not he who waits the slow decay
    Of sickness or decrepid age
Counting the long, long, listless days
    That no benignant views engage.

No: but the man whose generous soul
    Glows with the love of human kind;

> Who, pressing on to Freedom's goal,
>   Casts every selfish thought behind.

> 'Tis he—the Patriot—honoured name!
>   Blest with a heart that cannot fear,
> May best the proud distinction claim
>   Of solid bliss, and joy sincere.

Mr. Thelwell sometimes enriched his declamation by a bright impromptu. Alluding to the engrossed, the apathetic feeling of men engrossed in trade as having minds unsentimental

> "Ye slaves to business! bodies without soul!
> Important blanks in Nature's mighty whole."

and not infrequently introduced verse to give an impressive close to a wrought up scene as he did in the above pourtractiere of the artisan's wife on her way to the pawnbroker's vortex.

> Behold her
> In squalid clothes, with holes and gaping rent,
> With breaking heart, with trembling steps she went.

Were the subject to be thus left I should not do justice to it, nor to the reader. I do not doubt that individuals might be found, who would in a great degree answer to his portrait painting, but the general complexion of the country was, a state of morbid abundance, as a spendthrift prodigal manifests who is spending the income of several years in one, thus did our government for the state borrow immense sums at so low a rate as 56 for £100 3 per cent stock in the public funds. The war with France above

130,000,000 and in one sad year 60 millions of it. By such irrational national expenditure every article rose in price and the people were in great measure contented with the war, unmindful, that the borrowed sums were to be repaid at nearly double the price of the sum received. This is our case now 1849; the very sum borrowed at 56 is now 93 per cent. For the expenditure of these years and after years until 1814 was so great that the present debt is £800,000,000 and demands a payment of interest for a week £500,000 being about £26,000,000 annually.

In this year 1797 there remains yet two national calamities to be narrated which occurred within three months of each other. The first to be named is the mutiny of our Navy at the Nose, which stopped all waterborne supplies to the metropolis, and created a despondency and dread unequalled from any event in my previous days. The manner of manning the Navy by forcible impressment, their niggardly wages, their salt and inferior provisions being joined with a bashaw sort of rule in which some officers indulged in, led to the mutiny and those officers hastened the crisis by punishing the men with the lash for trivial offences. It is most worthy of remark and worthy of grateful remembrance that the crews did not ill use their officers or were disposed to fraternise with the enemy; they were still British tars: it was this very year that Lord Duncan's great victory: and my own victory calling Eunice mine. The seamen only required better pay, better food and better treatment and these were conceded to them. The principal Parker was executed.

In consequence of the stoppage of cash payments there was required a large increased issue of notes and such abundance of paper money in circulation still nourished the increase of prices. Gold was much hidden by the possessors, indeed it went nearly out of circulation, every stray guinea found its way to money dealers, who sold it again to the government for subsidies and payment of the Forces on the Continent. This change of paper for gold circulation as I have above informed, was at first, by order of Council but soon after an act of Parliament declared gold and notes equal in value, a tender of bank notes to be a legal tender—an unsupported assumption.

An incident occurred to me that may be worth relating as it vividly shows some of the effects that followed the enlarged issue of bank notes and releasing them from cash repayment. A customer of mine Mr. Horsey of Portsmouth owed £5 18s. 10d. which I wrote to him for payment. He replied that he had paid the amount and gave a very accurate statement; he said it was in a £5 note giving the date and number and the 18s. 10d. silver and copper and that it was sent in the parcel which contained a set of Henry's Bible sent to be bound. His statement was irresistibly true though his account had no credit for such payment but a credit was at that date given to the account opened to "Anonymous" of 18s. 10d. but not £5 18s. 10d. What had become of the £5 note was to be ascertained. Having the number and date, I went to the Bank and found it had been brought by a Mr. Thomas an eminent bullion dealer residing in Bank Buildings. Mr. T. stated he received it from Mr. xxxx in Liquor Pond Street. I found he kept a wretched chandler's shop and told me he *bought* it of the collector of Meux's Brewery. From him I learned that he had received it from a publican in Drury Lane, who stated that it was paid to him by a Jew clothes-man, a few doors distant. The Jew was honest and frank: he said, "I do not know the name of the person who paid it to me," but he so described a lad that, joining the description with the fact of its connection with a book to be bound, I charged the bookbinders' boy with embezzlement. He confessed his guilt and said, "I found the packet in a set of Henry's Bible sent to be bound. I took the £5 and gave you only 18s. 10d." which sum I, not knowing from whom it came, had put to an account under "Anonymous". Each of the persons who had possessed this note after the Jew and the publican had sold it and realised a profit until it came to Mr. Thomas who had given £6 10s. 0d. for it, in a new £5, a new £1 note and two dollars

| £ | s. | d. |
|---|----|----|
| 5 | 0 | 0 |
| 1 | 0 | 0 |
| 10 | 0 |
| £6 10 0 |

With minute accuracy I took down on paper, names and sales and deeming it right to communicate the result to the Bank, I had an interview with Mr. Hase, the Accountant General, who said, the Directors would sit in an hour and he would introduce me to explain personally what I had so clearly communicated. At the appointed time I was again with Mr. Hase who then said, "I have only to thank you but if people will give more for a bank-note than its value, they, the Bank, have no reason to complain." This reply was so perplexing to me, that I parted abruptly from Mr. Hase, with scarce due courtesy (of which he possessed very little for he stood erect stiff and with his hat on).

My perplexity oppressed my mind, the affair was so ambiguous that I was absorbed in thought and resolved to unravel the enigma. I did so, and with my new light went back to Mr. Hase. "Sir! your remark of a gain is futile, there is a *loss* to the exact amount of the apparent gain" and having explained my views, said he, "You are right but we cannot help it." The simple fact was that the very £5 bank note was not included in the restriction of it, being of more early date and therefore claimed gold payment. Mr. Thomas paid £6 10s. 0d. and he sold the gold it produced for 28s. that is £7 realising 10s. on every such £5 note and Mr. Hase said Mr. Thomas many days brought twenty or more such bank-notes. It is plain that the £7 would produce a deterioration of £2 in every seven, comparing gold with bank notes.

But to return to my narrative, our married life was soon clouded over by the failure of my health; though always delicate it now gave way so much that a visit to the country was deemed necessary and in September, 1798, my dear parents accompanied me to Englefield Green, a charming spot adjoining to Windsor Great Park, my dear wife remaining housekeeper at home. The letters that passed between us have been preserved by my wife and these letters on our first separation are in the possession of my dear daughter Eunice.

Our first sorrow had been the loss of our first born by the premature confinement of my dear wife on June 26th, 1798, but my illness was to her even a more severe trial, especially as the care of business rested on her during my absence. I returned home revived in health the end of October, my dear wife having visited us during the time.

On May 18th in the next year, 1799, I embraced a dear sweet boy whom I named Samuel; he died the December following in consequence of smallpox inoculation, then the general practice. He was inoculated from his cousin George a fine healthy child a few months older than himself. The dear child had the experiment tried by medical advice of checking the disease by exposure to the air. The consequence was, as I have said, fatal, and after a most distressing illness in which only one great pock appeared on the foot he expired on December 21st, 1799, and was buried on Christmas day following in his grandfather Birch's tomb in Tottenham Court Chapel.

In August, 1800, I was again obliged to go from home for my health and at this time it was to Margate. My dear parents came to see me there but whether the trip was beneficial or not I do not remember. My chief resort was to the gardens of a house, once the residence of a family whose crest was a grotesque heraldic lion with teeth above nature and the figures were in stone at the entrance pillars of the gate. It was once called Dents des Lions which sunk in common vogue into Dandelion House.

In October (19th) of that year my third son was born. He lived to be thirty-five years of age and died on July 1st, 1835, of a painful tumour occasioned by a slight accident in his early years. At the time it occurred he had very skilful attention but his medical man on parting said he may feel this thirty years hence. This circumstance my dear wife did not remember until after his death, and it was then recalled to her memory by a relative to whom Samuel went to school in his earliest years. She remembers the injunction respecting him and the medical opinion expressed. Mr. Frogly, the medical gentleman who attended my Samuel during his long painful and last illness was much perplexed as to the *cause* of my son's disease in one so temperate in his habits and we much regretted that the foregoing circumstance was not brought to our memory while we had an opportunity of explaining it.

In October, 1795, my most worthy grandfather George Bagster died at Lyme aged eighty-seven years. He was of an affectionate disposition, his love to my grandmother was strong and abiding, long after her death, several years after her death, he had been known to rise from his bed and pace the room moaning "O my dear Alice! my dear Alice!" She died in 1782 thirteen years before him, aged 78 years. She surpassed most in beauty. She was a fine tall woman and the grace of her natural movement well harmonised with her amiability of disposition. She had eyes black as the raven and a countenance bright and expressive. My grandfather was fair, his eyes blue gray and his hair light brown. The elder of these two sons (my father) followed his father and the younger son resembled the mother and in the following generation the two families have similarly been distinct in their complexions and colour of eyes and hair, my uncle James' family having the fine sparkling black eyes of my grandmother which he inherited from her while most of our side of the house are fair and have light eyes and hair.

About this time the first carriage in the shape of an omnibus ran, it had eight wheels, plying between Southampton and London. It went one day and returned the next, not running on the Sunday. Now 3,000 run in London. This fourth era, completing the century, may with propriety be closed by noticing the continued loss of seconds each year which at this time amounting to a day, this year 1800 though leap year the month of February had but 28 days as that February will also in the year 1900 but in the year 2000 will again be a leap year. When the new style put aside the old style in 1752 the calendar lost eleven days, thus September 3rd was called September 14th and in this year one other day was lost, whereby between 1752 and 1800 assimilated the styles but between 1800 and 1900 twelve days are required to reconcile the styles. Those of my readers who are acquainted with the writings of Steel and Addison in the *Tatler* and *Spectator* will surely have noticed that two dates are placed to such numbers as appeared between January 1st, and March

25th and thus it was always adopted in letters because the year began in England March 26th and in other places generally on January 1st, and since 1752 the year commences universally on January 1st, and the new style is adopted throughout Europe, except in Russia and by the Greek Church.

# 1800 - 1807

At the commencement of this fifth septennary division of my life, the clouds were heavy and threatened yet deeper darkness. The state of my health was increasingly discouraging giving but little hope of the long continuance of my life. The symptoms were considered indicative of incipient consumption and I was medically recommended to go to the Hotwells at Bristol. The step was considered necessary for my life and it was concluded to be effected with all promptness. The plan arranged was, that I should meet my father at Lyme as he returned from his annual western journey and after spending a few days with him there to proceed from thence to Bristol. At Lyme there was now no tender active aunt Edwards, no aged grandfather to give me welcome; their removal by death left me homeless at Lyme and at an inn I took up my abode. When my father arrived, in every way he shewed his paternal love and sympathy, he consulted Dr. Carpenter of Lyme and Dr. Robinson of Honiton, both eminent in the circle of their practice. I accompanied my father to Axminster to visit Mr. Whitty, the manufacturer of the "Axminster Carpets", who had brought that branch of trade to lofty eminence. Mr. Whitty was the maker of that grand display of skill, the great carpet of the music room at Carlton House whereon was exhibited all the instruments of various ages and nations. The cost of production was very considerable from the good quality of the wool and of the dye and the difficulty of covering so large a space in one piece.

On Sunday we rode from Lyme to Axminster to attend

the morning service with Mr. Whitty and dined with the friendly man and in the evening again returned to our quarters at Lyme. On Monday we proposed to travel to Chard on our way to Bristol (the Bristol and Exeter coach passing through that town) but by the fatigue on Sunday I was more unwell on the next day. Dr. Carpenter paid me a visit and he deemed it proper for me to lose blood; he bled me and gave his opinion the ride to Chard would not be injurious. My dear father hired a post chaise to convey us there and on our passing through Axminster, which is on the road mid-way between Lyme and Chard, we had the sad information of Mr. Whitty's sudden decease, he being seized with apoplexy a few hours after we left him. The surprise and shock received increased effect by our prospects as to my health and by our so recent friendly intercourse with him. On entering the chaise I placed myself against the back leaning into the corner, out of that position I did not move the two hours of the journey but when we arrived at the inn at Chard on my descending from the chaise I found myself weak from loss of blood, the bandage had slipped, I had lost so much that my clothes were saturated. When I had become calm at the inn, I recovered my tone and after a night's rest was able to think of my journey by coach to Bristol but my kind liberal father would not allow me to go by the coach but posted it all the way to the Hotwells. My father had previously requested Mr. Isaac Nash of Bristol to provide a suitable lodging for us and he engaged one in the house of Mrs. Pope, No. 2 Dawry Parade on the ground floor. The ground floor had been prefered—it was injurious for persons with pulmonary symptoms to go upstairs. The preceding inhabitant of these rooms was Miss Trelawny (eldest daughter of Sir Harry Trelawney) who died therein, notwithstanding the utmost skill, regardless of cost, which had been incurred with the fallacious hope of cure. The floor of the room, a large room, in which I slept, was considerably damaged and on enquiry into the cause was informed that Miss Trelawny under the advice of the eminent Dr. Beddoes had cows fastened by staples to the floor so that the cows breathed into the young lady's face, who, necessarily, by each inspiration of her breath inhaled the breath of the animal. Dr. Beddoes was a considerable experimenter on medical air, and the use of gases in the cure of diseases, and has written and published much on the subject. I confess and record my opinion, that the vaccine breath experiment deserved only contempt, unworthy of any man of sane understanding. Though Dr. Beddoes was the popular physician I escape being a victim to his scheming. I was attended by Dr. Fox, a man of very benignant stamp of character; he treated me, as all were then treated who were consumptive or supposed to be so, with repeated doses of Digit. Purp. to continually keep a nausea in the stomach but so as not to excite vomiting. This medicine has the power of reducing the pulse but I found it created a feeling of sinking and fainting. Had Dr. Carpenter or Dr. Fox been sagacious enough to ascertain what my *natural* pulse counted (my pulse being naturally very high) he would not have taken blood away nor Dr. Fox have administered the Fox Glove and I should have been saved from much suffering. The dietary ordered was of a quality to lower the pulse and physical powers. No animal food was allowed but a constant use of baked apples. I actually hated the sight of the vessel that contained the apples. Dr. Fox happened one day to ask my good father if he had any other child than me, and learning that he had several, expressed great surprise. "I felt confident," said he, "you had only this child by the unusual anxiety you express for his health."

Dr. Fox did for a few years afterwards pay me a visit on his annual arrival in town. My dear mother soon arrived and stayed with me until my return home. By the baronetage I learn that Miss Trelawny's name was Anne Letitia, born January 27th, 1779, this young lady must have been in her twenty-second year.

How long I was at the Hotwells memory leaves no record, but I returned home in no better condition than when I left. My dear wife then proposed I should take the advice of Mr. Chevalier a medical friend of my wife's family, he was consulted and explicitly gave it as his confident opinion that I was in no danger of a consumption; that I needed a liberal supply of food, that a beef steak once, even twice a day would do me good. The use of the cold bath he recommended and a hair mattress instead of a bed. This advice harmonised with my opinion of my wants. My stomach was very willing to be eased of nausea by the Digit. Purp. and constantly having by the repetition of apples my palate nauseated at the food, therefore stomach and palate hailed the exchange of beef instead of apples. My father objected warmly and affectionately against the use of the cold bath. "What! with this cough to go into the cold bath!" His earnestness evidenced his love but Mr. Chevalier's advice I had the courage to follow and my health speedily became wondrously amended. I became indeed as strong as my constitution admitted my frame to be.

Not recollecting the exact period in which the following transaction occurred, I record it in this fifth era of my days, at the same time considering that perhaps the preceding era had a greater claim to its introduction.

Anthony Brown, Esq., the agent for the Legislature of the Island of Antigua applied to me to arrange, methodise and index the laws in practice in that island which had not thereto been printed. The laws were in MS, were loose in a rough box, in a disarranged state in no chronological order, many on half sheets of paper. I secured a suitable person and the whole was executed to Mr. Brown's satisfaction and I received the thanks of the Legislature from the Speaker. The work formed two volumes quarto, the whole impression was bound in Russian leather to preserve them from cockroaches and ants, the odour of that leather repels them. In the progress of arrangement frequent appeals were made to me as to the partial or entire repeal of some of the acts. The editor asked, "Sir, two slaves have been pilfering. I desire to know whether they are to be scourged or hanged for I have two acts alike; except as to punishment, one gives the lash, the other hangs." The reader will be at no loss to conclude which was dismissed. The whole cost was less than £1,000. On their passage to the island, the vessel was captured by a French privateer and carried into Guadaloupe. The governor of Antigua despatched a flag of truce to the French governor of Guadaloupe, requesting the restitution of the cases of books, because they were "The Laws of the Island". The French governor replied he would answer by his own flag of truce and the result was favourable and very honourable to the French governor. The cases of books were sent, not lacking one, with a communication that it was a gratification to restore them, for he did not see it as a right use of war to oppose moral improvement.

To pay the expenses of the truce, as the shipper I was called upon to pay and the underwriters who had insured the goods refusing, I did so and at the expense of thirty pounds.

The year 1801 introduced me to the acquaintance of Mr. Daniel Terry. He became a celebrated actor, and had literary talents; he obtained the warm friendship of Sir Walter Scott who lent him a considerable sum to enable him to join Mr. Yates in the purchase of the Adelphi Theatre. This plan fell, in the ruin of Constable & Co.'s bankruptcy in 1825. The author and the bookseller had created accommodation bills to the large sum of £120,000, and Mr. Terry was compelled to pay the sum he had borrowed of the baronet, as part of the estate the creditors claimed. This ruined Mr. Terry, drove him to the Continent, where mental anxiety broke down his health and he languished in poverty until 1828, when he died, as is commonly called, of a broken heart. Mr. Terry is introduced into this chit chat narrative in order to narrate the singular mode he adopted to qualify himself for the stage. He then occupied two rooms in Cliffords Inn. I called on him to obtain payment of my account for books supplied to him (he was a great book buyer). I found him in bed, in a small room lined with shelves, full of books, which were chiefly within his reach: the room was lightened by a candle placed on a large book on the bed, the daylight excluded by shutters. "Why, Mr. Terry! I hope you are not ill." "O dear no, I enjoy reading by candlelight." As I went out the female attendant said that he had continued day and night for a fortnight and read incessantly, seeming to take no sleep. This seclusion was to accomplish his intentions to add mental pregnancy of knowledge, as a needful qualification for the higher walk of theatrical representation.

> Terry! Once, saw I, thy strange acumen,
> Gathering solar light by candle lumen,
>     For thy enlarg'd tuition!
> Great Actor! When to thy high stature grown,
> And didst Nature court—She, thy suit did own,
>     Securing thy fruition!

No more of this friend of Scott—I lament his end.

I have an anecdote to tell of a man who was for a time notoriously popular, a short time before this period. His popularity was much greater in America, his scepticism and vicious republicanism did not find the English so congenial for its growth. Enter Thomas Payne. He was by trade a staymaker, and as a staymaker, worked in the shop of Mr. Northam (of Southampton Buildings, Holborn) a worthy man, intimate with our family, who told it to my father. There is no doubt of the truth of the anecdote. Paine's vivacity and ready wit, marked him as one who would claim the notice of all his fellow workmen. He was habitually slovenly in his dress and negligent of his personal appearance: but one day came in very differently dressed, clean shaved, clean linen and well attired. This unusual smartness called forth all the jokes and jibes of his fellow workmen. "Why, Tom, you are surely going to be married!" Afterwards he admitted that it was to be the case next day and said he liked a day before to flourish in his wedding clothes. Another remarked the smartness of his legs and their fair proportions, and said, "Tom! they are cork calves!" This he stiffly denied, but while so denying, one and another stuck pins into the cork and then called Mr. Payne's attention to the fact of these helps to his beauty. Not feeling the pins was a proof they did not enter flesh. This man resigned himself to intemperate habits, but yet life continued until 1809, and on his death, he desired to be buried in the quaker's burial grounds. This, the friends refused, because of his deistical sentiments and he was buried in his own garden; and Cobbett in 1817 went to America, and asserted on his return to this country that he had disinterred the bones of Paine and brought them with him. The fact has been contradicted by a report that he did not take that trouble but brought home a malefactor's bones that had been executed. It is of little consequence which is right. William Cobbett was the most remarkable man of this age for brilliant intellect and practical utilitarianism, a violent political writer, but his ultra-ardour will find apologists, but his sad perversion of truth in a work he called "A History of the Reformation" has left an endurable tarnish on his name. He died in the year 1835, being then M.P. for Oldham.

In 1802 the whole nation was convulsed with joy at a peace between France and England, signed at Amiens, but the reflecting portion of the British nation considered it more as a truce to gather strength, rather than a substantial settlement. The event was eminently a blessing to numerous families who had relatives confined in France, and they were many.

Buonaparte's conduct towards the English was faithless and violent. He did by a tyrannical order put all Englishmen under arrest who were then for pleasure or for purposes of commerce, travelling in France. They were not generally confined in prison but compelled to live in a town, within the bounds of a fortress and the larger number were in the garrison town of Verdun. Several of these sufferers I knew, of whom two I only will name. Captain Wilson, the husband of Mr. Summers' second daughter, Mary; sister to my brother George's wife Sarah. This Captain Wilson was one. Captain Wilson after about two years confinement made his escape home in a cart, having trays of crockery ware suspended over him. He thus reached Holland and arrived safely long before the peace. The other case was pitiable, it was my neighbour Payne, the bookseller (who was in partnership with McKinlay) whose spirits and health failed and he died and his partner was overwhelmed and drowned himself in Paddington canal. Both perished.

But in some former page I have expressed deep regret

at the number of executions for robberies and forgeries. England was herein more sanguinary in its punishments than any other nation. Having conscientiously entertained the opinion of the impropriety of such executions, except for the crime of murder, holding that opinion, to have witnessed one would have been a horror but an atrocious murder had been committed on the person of Mr. Steele of Catherine Street, Strand (whom I personally knew) a chemist of fame, founded on his successful distillation of Lavender-Water. He cultivated the plant on a portion of Hounslow Heath and frequently visited the plantation. As he, on one such visit was crossing the heath he was brutally murdered. Few cases, even of murder, have excited so intense an interest as this. Two men were tried and were found guilty. They both were agricultural labourers, their names Holloway and Haggerty. The proof against the latter could not be doubted but against the former, I think only two circumstances evincing his guilt were produced. He was on the Heath, on the borders of which he lived, about the supposed time, and, one boot of Mr. Steel's was taken off and was found under his bedstead, the other being left on the person of Mr. Steele. The executions were no longer at Tyburn, but took place in the Old Bailey opposite the debtor's door of Newgate Prison. My brother in Law, Mr. Prosser, asked me to accompany him to a house opposite to view from thence the dreadful scene. As the punishment of death appeared proper for such a crime, I did not hesitate to accompany him. We were at a window immediately opposite and nearly on a level of the platform on which the culprits stood and we could see all that passed distinctly and hear all that was spoken in any degree higher or more emphatic than colloquial talk. The whole circumstances of the case and the trial, had produced such an intensity of feeling, that myriads were present, the whole street was full and closely packed. Such an assembly of sightseers, had not on any previous occasion been collected. The unhappy sufferers came on to the scaffold attended by the usual officers. The executioner, chaplain, etc. Haggerty was a man below the middle stature and did not raise his head and was first placed on the fatal plank; a woman for the murder of a sailor by stabbing him in the eye was placed next him. Holloway was a fine powerful man, little if any, short of six feet, of full open countenance. The hangman was about to place him on the plank next to the woman when he gently resisted and came to the railing of the scaffold, and, standing firmly up, said, with plain unbroken sonorous voice, apparently undaunted, as an innocent man would act upheld by conscious innocency. "I am innocent, Gentlemen! Innocent! Innocent!" I thought he did as well as his pinioned arms would allow; appeared to wish to raise them in an appeal to God—so it appeared to me. He then with a firm step walked across the platform on the opposite side and with equal clearness and loudness said the same words, after which he returned to the place the executioner was about to place him, and said to him in an unimpassioned tone and unruffled manner, "Do I stand right?" The bolt was drawn and life speedily ended but the painful impression was fixt in my mind, that Holloway was not guilty and suffered being innocent.

This execution was attended with a direful catastrophe. The multitude appeared, to us who looked on them from above, to rock to and fro, like undulated waves of a quiet sea when gently heaved by the rising tide. A space had been parted off by rails and posts for the occupation of the attending constables and they had admitted a man within that enclosure with a basket of hot pies. One of these waving rolls of the close packed immense mass, by its weight broke the chain or a post gave way. The persons near fell over the pieman's basket and the extraordinary result of this sudden increase of room was that so many struggled for relief from pressure, ignorant of the accidental death of some that a mound of people one on another was raised and continued to increase, until some were actually taken in at a one pair window!—and when the heaped up sufferers removed or were removed, twenty-eight persons perished!—amongst whom were the next door neighbour to Mr. Birch, Angel Row, Hammersmith, and his eldest son. The dead bodies were in a row placed in St. Sepulchre's vestry to be identified, and as they were owned, the name was put on a label and pinned on the clothes of the body.

On June 27th, 1802, my fourth son John was born.

On April 29th, 1804, my first girl was born whom we named after her mother. My dear son John was not like his elder brother, Samuel, of robust health. He was, soon after the birth of our little Eunice, attacked with a dangerous illness which terminated in putrid fever. It was thought desirable that he should have a change of air and my dear wife went to Hastings with him and Samuel and the baby. Mrs. Chevalier, the wife of our esteemed medical attendant wishing to visit the sea side at the same time it was agreed that my wife and her three children and Mrs. Chevalier and her four children should reside there together. The two husbands accompanied the wives down and saw them comfortably settled in lodgings open to the sea but eccentricities of this lady rendered the arrangement less agreeable than was anticipated, and, my dear wife, to insure the continuance of the friendship between the families, sought another lodging. Mr. Chevalier most kindly apologised on his wife's behalf and said he trusted that nothing would be allowed to lessen my wife's regard to Mrs. Chevalier and Mrs. Chevalier herself was ill soon after her return and, not expecting to live, sent for my dear wife and solemnly committed all her children to her trust. The letters that passed on this circumstance between me and my wife yet remain.

One historical reminiscence connected with that period and our residence at Hastings is worth noticing here. An invasion of England was apprehended. The flotilla and troops provided on the opposite coast, did, for magnitude, place the Spanish Armada in the shadow and from the character of Buonaparte's constitution of mind, it was suggested, and expected to give an effect, that he would land on the spot where the victorious Norman had landed in 1066. Beyond the fact of his ultimate triumph, his landing has a halo of heroism about it. As soon as his troops were landed, he burned all the ships, and said to his troops, "See Your Country." Hastings was therefore a place where the invasion assumed a tone of reality and some dread. In one letter I charge my wife not to part with five guineas *in gold*, because she might need them should a sudden flight from that town become necessary. Paper currency rendered "Gold" more effective in payment in a period of public excitement.

As I am not writing the incidents of my progress through life in any strict chronological order, I may indulge in an episode occasionally, especially when an opportunity offers by it of exhibiting my cleverness! When in my shop alone and about this period, I heard a bitter cry in the next house, then under repair. I rushed in and found in the one pair room an Irish labourer seated on a heap of bricks groaning and bleeding. I instantly saw the occasion of his cry. He had been pulling down a part of a stack of chimney-jamb and underpicking it to let it fall in mass, and

so it did but he was too near. It took in its fall the brawny
calf of his leg which was torn and hung down towards his
heel. I with promptness lifted up the great lump of flesh
placed it in the best order I could, and, with my neckcloth
and handkerchief, bound up the leg. A messenger was sent
for Mr. Jones, a neighbouring surgeon, who recommended
his immediate removal to St. George's Hospital. Mr. Jones
gave me a large phial of brandy and water in case he
should faint in the coach. "But," said he, "by no means
give him a drop unless he is fainting." I went with the
man to the hospital and got him safely in. The flesh had
been well placed and the wrapping as well done that the
surgeons thought it better to leave the leg to the process
of nature and the restoration became so perfect that the
poor fellow was encouraged to come, after he was out of
hospital, on days of the pupils assembling at lecture, to
show his leg to exemplify the power of nature in performing a perfect cure, even almost seamless.

On December 9th, 1805, my dear son Augustus was
born. The short record of this boy is melancholy. He was
truly a beautiful child, docile and sweet. He had attained
the age of twenty months, when his dear mother, who was
hourly expecting to present me with another child,
sent him out to walk with his sister Eunice and the nurse-
maid in Somerset House, airy and open to the river. The
iron railings (since in consequence altered) to the deep
areas were then very wide apart, wide enough for a child
to creep through. The maid (Ann Messenger by name)
had got acquaintance with a footman in Somerset House
and while conversing with him, forgot the dear children.
They, Eunice and Augustus, were amusing themselves on
one of the broad stones to an entrance, watching a man
beating a coat on a stand, when the little darling crept
through, fell down the area and was taken up insensible,

the skull being fractured. The beadle of the parish first informed me, in a true official unfeeling way. I hastened to the place and found my dear boy lying on the table of a surgeon, who lived near to the place of the accident. The surgeon had attempted to bleed him but in vain. A few minutes after my arrival the dear babe breathed his last. His body was conveyed home soon after.

While I was from home on this melancholy occasion a dear little girl was born. This was on August 14th, 1807. We named her Augusta in memory of her little brother, whose death happened at the hour of her birth. My sorrow at the calamitous death of the dear child had thereto much pungency added, lest the event should have a bad effect on my dear wife in her then weak state. The concealing of it from her for a few days was accomplished by my sister-in-law, Sarah, asking the other children to spend a few days with her and thus a fit time and suitable manner being chosen, the loss was born without the apprehended evils.

In 1806, I very satisfactorily accomplished an object I had long designed, to possess portraits of my parents and of my wife's parents. The artist I employed was Mr. Charles Hayter (the father of the present Sir George Hayter) who has admirably succeeded—each one is faithfully correct and has the right expression.

My Father, George Bagster, born July 19th, 1739 O.S.
aged 67.
My Mother, Mary Bagster, born May 6th, 1738, O.S.
aged 68.
My Father-in-law, John Birch, born Feb. 24th, 1738 O.S.
aged 68.
My Mother-in-law, Charlotte Birch, born March 17th, 1742,
O.S. aged 64.

These dates are under the *autograph* signatures at the

back of this loving assemblage. They were each worthy of honourable remembrance. My dear wife and I occupy the centre square of the picture with our son Samuel, between us, then six years of age.

In 1807, an enterprising man of the name of Winsor proposed to light London and Westminster with gas and had formed a company to carry the plan into effect and while the bill was in its progress, he erected iron pillars with gas lights every fifty feet on one side of Pall Mall and truly was it a blaze of light. The Bill to give him adequate power to carry his plan into effect did not pass and the day after its rejection, I saw a host of workmen removing this range of pillars. Gas did not get into general use until 1814.

A little incident in connection with it I will mention. My daughter Eunice, when home for the Easter Holidays, I invited out to see the bright effect. As we passed a silversmith's shop in the Strand, near to Temple Bar, she exclaimed, "There is a large gas-light, Papa, in the kitchen." I saw the occasion, a curtain had taken fire. I dashed my hand through the glass and pulled down the burning curtain and gave notice in the shop of the great danger.

# 1807 - 1814

The sixth of the eleven divisions of my life from 1807 to 1814: the age of thirty-six to forty-three.

In 1809, August 12th, my dear auburn headed Charlotte was born. We named her after her grandmother Birch.

It was in this year the direful war with France raged in its intensity. An English force was despatched to Holland under the command of the Duke of York to save that country from French occupation. The Duke was driven to great straits. The dykes were opened to flood the country that the progress of the French army might be impeded; the step highly injurious to the country but needful for the preservation of the British troops. This step did not avail, in consequence of an extraordinarily severe frost, which increased the danger and brought our army into the greatest peril. Their capture or destruction seemed inevitable and the capture of the Royal Duke himself. The flat island of Walcheren was a refuge. When the frost ceased, rain accompanied the thaw, which put that low flat island into a condition of great misery to the English troops,—no barracks, no cover, nothing but ditches and wet surface. That dismal island, at that season, was a mere swamp. The army suffered great loss by a low strength-devouring fever called the Walcheren fever. My brother William (who was Dep. Com. Gen.) was on duty with the army and was attacked by the prevalent low fever, of which so very many died. He survived the attack but never fully attained his former state of health.

The Duke of York sent the most vehement demands for a reinforcement of his army, requiring all the troops that could be possibly despatched and urged the greatest speed in sending them. The War Office energetically complied with the urgent requisition. It happened that I became so situated, as to witness one of the measures which this exigency made necessary. I was proceeding on business to see Mr. Arnet of Salisbury and took my place as an outside passenger by the Exeter coach. I noticed the peculiarity that the horses were not changed, as usual, at the town of Hounslow, but I made no remark to the coachman or to my fellow travellers. A second peculiarity occurred, about a mile westward from that town. The coachman drew the coach off the turnpike road on to the turf, some distance, a furlong or so, and there were the horses, grooms, ready for changing. Our tired horses were removed and fresh ones put to the coach and we returned on to the turnpike again. The coachman drove rather slower than the usual pace, and, so it was, that although several appearances might have raised the propriety of enquiry what it all meant, I did not ask. The coach proceeded in this calm pace about two miles or less, when we arrived near to a place in the road where some troops and a considerable number of single horse country carts without horses and a single row of these empty carts, placed close to each other across the road. A little distance before we reached this place, the coachman suddenly became all energy, shook the reins, stamped his feet and urged the horses to speed with all the exciting tones of his experienced voice—to excite the animals to effort and speed; an imagination let loose would transport himself to the spectacles of Rome, where the horses wild from Arabia, run free; it would not exceed the new burst of energy of these four fine young horses, picked out from his great stock for this feat. The proprietor had selected these, full fed and courageous.

The man of the whip too singled out for the enterprise, the cattle experienced his ability. The effect was singular, all were taken by surprise. The great force suddenly made against these carts by the leaders, separated them, upsetting one or more and dashing between them. Almost before the feat was done I saw the sudden adventure had raised an effort of the soldiers to mount their horses and hinder or overtake the coach. The troopers followed certainly, but the coachman said, "I will defy them with such *beauties* before me to overtake us, and in fact by their unpreparedness for such conduct and thereby waiting a minute or two to mount their horses, we had got ahead and to what extent they made chase I did not observe, but we escaped the danger (which was considerable) and the inconvenience of being left in the road to find a conveyance as we could. The coachman had orders from the proprietors of the coach, at all risks to pass the barriers and not be stopped. How true I cannot say but on the road it was stated that so absolute were the orders to spare none, that Mrs. Abbot, the Speaker's lady, had her horses taken from the carriage. I found in this exciting scene my attention was more fixed on the single point of the coachman's heroism and skill than on the danger we were in. I felt no dread, probably not through moral courage but the danger and the escape came so close together, that there was no interval for thought or fear.

Having told my readers of one adventurous scene, I will introduce to the readers' lively attention a threatening danger: beyond Buonaparte's invasion, or, equestrian exploits, the reader may contemplate the threatened destruction of the world, by the collision of a comet with our planet. This was painfully apprehended in 1811.

Then appeared a comet of great size,* visible to the naked eye every evening at sunset, and, every evening it was gazed at, by myriads and was regarded as a phenomenon foreboding future evils and present destruction. The fears though groundless were painful to many. The apprehension of the million were deepened by contrary opinions of men of science, as to the perihelion† of the comet and its nearness to the earth; these were subjects of correspondence in the daily papers. That it was supposed to be so near the earth as to cause the heat and stillness of atmosphere. The perpendicular fissures were unusually gaping and deep.

It became almost an annual custom to take the children to the seaside during the midsummer vacation. In the year 1812 the visit was to Hastings, of which my lively, cheerful wife wrote a journal, which is yet in existence.

> Delineations there are true and sweet
>> From her warm heart and graphic pen—
> My precious children found it such a treat
>> They wish'd next year it might come o'er again.

Sister Sarah, my brother George's wife, between whom and my dear wife the sweetest love always subsisted, went this time, with my wife with all their and our children. My brother George and I going down as often as business allowed, generally on a Saturday and home again on Monday. I will name only one little adventure of donkeys. We had a donkey squadron to visit Winchelsea, its castle and mere. The distance about nine miles, our muster was

---

* Sir John Herschel says, "The train of light, with which most comets are accompanied, is called the tail." The tail of the comet of 1769 extended 16,000,000 leagues and that of the great comet of 1811 36,000,000.

† Perihelion, is the point in the orbit of a comet nearest the sun.

nine donkeys and two mules, which finished little to our satisfaction, for, the donkey juvenile drivers got tipsy and we had to take a post chaise to convey the little ones and the weak ones to our home again. As I believe my wife's journal gives a better account of this adventure, I dismiss it and other incidents of this marine jaunt.

In the year 1811, June 23rd, my dear Benjamin was born and in the year 1813, January 28th, my dear Jonathan was born. It was in 1811 Great Britain was convulsed by the assassination of the Prime Minister of England, Spencer Percival Esquire, as he entered the lobby of the House of Commons by a man named Bellingham, who intended to have shot Lord Levison Gower but killed Mr. Percival mistaking one for the other.

With a smile now on my face, which remembrance brings, I will insert a droll occurrence occasioned by a misapprehension of a common idiom of colloquial speech; if it makes the reader smile also, my trouble of writing it will be recompensed. In the anecdote, there is no punning (the lowest class of witticisms) but there is grace and pleasantry because it was *real*; and, the eliptical use of one word had brought into the familiarity of idiomatic language. Mr. John Murray (with whom I was a schoolfellow for a short time) then of Fleet Street and afterwards of wide celebrity as a publisher in Albemarle Street, had offered some books for my purchase. The offer was not acceptable to me and on my return from the city, I called to see Mr. Murray to have personally explained my resignation of his offer; he being absent, I went to his desk at the end of the shop and wrote on his blotting paper "Finding you out—I decline your offer, S.B." or to that effect. Not long after, being at dinner with my family in the parlour at the back of the shop, the door was hastily opened and in came Mr. Murray flushed, and looking eagerly at me said somewhat loudly "Pray Sir! What have you found me out in doing?" I saw his blunder and calmly replied, "by 'finding you out' I intended only to say, finding you not in your house—that is, not at home." I was adding explanation, when he so quickly retired, that the whole comic scene had scarcely more than a minute's existence.

In the autumn of this year (1813) I took a journey to Beresford Hall in Staffordshire which I have in part written, and preferring to leave it separate from this personal narrative I herein dismiss the narration and to it refer the reader.

The year 1814 is memorable for the peace with France, won by the sword of British process and long may it continue! The proclamation of this peace was celebrated by a grand triumphant procession to St. Paul's to render public thanksgiving. The parks were illuminated and fun and fireworks were kept up all night. A bridge was built over the canal in the park from whence fireworks illuminated the cheerful scene, and boats rowed up and down the canal which amused many and it is pleasant to add that I did not see one person intoxicated or behaving unseemly.

> Hail, gentle Peace, with thy bright train!
> Sweet retinue of Bliss—to bless—
> Should cursed war arise again
> The world becomes a wilderness.

Thanks to the God of peace, the ruler of nations, it is yet peace and now in 1849 every prospect appears favourable for its continuance.

With peace and gratitude I close the sixth period of my life. One event more I will however add, that I, at this time had the promised blessing to the Jewish nation granted to me—for my children were truly as olive-branches around my table. This year, 1814 (?); January 27th, another son was added to my number, whom we named Cornelius Birch.

# 1814 - 1821

This seventh seventh period contains from the year 1814 to 1821—the forty-third to the fiftieth years of my age.

The year 1815 is memorable (and to Great Britain it will ever be) for that year sees the general conflict between England and France, or, more properly should I not say, the mighty struggle of principle was brought to close by the union of all the European powers being successful against France and the possession of Paris itself by the mighty mass of the combined armies.

The joy and boast of this country surpassed moderate bounds. The successful battle of Waterloo under the command of our Wellington, had gloriously ended the war. The direful destruction of men in the frozen plains of Russia had caused the British Nation to hope that Napoleon's power might be overthrown, yet the realization of that hope filled every bosom with transport now— freedom from the danger of invasion was secured and the whole future presented a bright hopeful prospect.

The conqueror of Nations, the distributor of thrones— a prisoner to the English, whom he had intended to destroy! To their destruction he had perseveringly directed the whole energy of his mighty mind and mighty power.

My dear children were taken out to see the fireworks and the illuminations. At this time I had in my service two very tall porters, both *above* six feet high, and loftily raised on their shoulders were two of my younger children seated and the rest with me. The displays were various and splendid P N M C puzzled us greatly, but after a time it was elucidated by one of my little youngsters and I now record that in particular as it is serviceable to exhibit the spirit of the rejoicings PROUD NAPOLEON MADE CAPTIVE. Gas was then first used as an illumination. The circle of it, with its running sparkling fire, then, was a great curiosity and attracted general admiration.

In 1816 I removed from the Strand to Paternoster Row. The general wonder of the year 1817 was the exploits of a reckless brutish indigent man, named Cummins, who urged by poverty and vulgar notoriety, became an object to be gazed at by the champing of stones, as though they were gingerbread nuts or biscuits, and not only following the practice of swallowing pebbles had the temerity to swallow clasp knives; by which he obtained a precarious support by the money payments of the spectators of his folly. Poor wretched Cummins! His death was not long deferred: it took place in Guy's Hospital and eighteen knives were found in his stomach and intestines. The knives, chiefly, were such as sailors use.

On my removal from the Strand into Paternoster Row we did not live at this place of business but resided in Lambeth Holb. Doctors Commons, where was born my youngest child on 23rd January, 1817, whom we named Ebenezer. He was not strong but appeared healthy and promising, but he did not thrive and after nine days existence he died on his mother's lap and so peacefully that for some time it was not clear whether he were dead or asleep.*

In the year 1819 my very dear and excellent father died of apoplexy on December the twenty-fourth. The circumstances of the attack were these. After dinner he was sitting with my dear mother, *in his usual fond* way with her, had drawn his chair away from its common position, by the side of the fire, and, because she was very deaf, had

* In 1817 wheat bore the famine price of £7.8.0 per quarter.

placed it close to her, opposite the fire. In addressing my mother, he began "lovey bird" (the familiar name of affection to her) and took her hand between his and began talking on bygone days, when suddenly, while speaking, fell forwards from his chair and struck his nose against the top bar of the grate. As quickly as possible, my dear mother dragged him back, rang the bell for assistance and medical aid was immediately called in and we, his children, were sent for. The usual remedy of bleeding was resorted to and with the usual result—my dear father recovered his senses in a considerable degree but did not long survive the loss of blood. He expired the third day after the attack without a sigh or a struggle. He was eighty years of age.

Happy did I feel that I had obtained a truthful miniature of him by Mr. Charles Hayter, which well expresses his beaming countenance when he had just finished a cheerful anecdote. I have *mental* memorial of his many noble qualities, which will never fade, but will and now does afford a theme I shall always delightfully dwell on. One single feature I will present to my readers, for which he was eminently distinguished. It was an enduring firmness in his friendships (and that of Mr. Bailey comes into the mind) and love. This won for him the wide respect which he obtained and which for many years rejoiced my heart to witness and is now a high pleasure to call to recollection. This attractive feature of his mind and heart begat not only a love to his family but spread an attachment to all relations.

The mortal remains of this dear parent were placed in my elder brother's grave in Bunhill Fields cemetery. Without previous notice and greatly to my surprise Christopher Idle, Esquire, M.P. for Weymouth and of the Adelphi Terrace, appointed me joint executor with Mr.

Brougham, his brother-in-law. The affairs were intricate and important and the duty was heavy on me for several years but at length the duty was fulfilled, the affairs closed and I have the satisfaction to hold, with expressed satisfaction, a full release by his only son surviving, Mr. Christopher Idle.

# 1821 - 1828

The eighth seventh division of my life—1821 to 1828—
being the forty-ninth to fifty-sixth years of my age.

This era shall be ushered in by noticing my presentation
at Court to his Majesty George IV by the Archbishop of
Canterbury (Sutton) to present a copy of the Book of
Common Prayer in eight languages which was received
in the King's usual graceful manner and I kissed his fat
white hand. He stood apparently on a cushion or
raised floor, he was certainly elevated above the nobles
around him, lofty and royal, he "looked every inch a
king". As I passed with a stream of people through the
ante-room to the Audience Chamber, I was addressed by
the friendly Lord Advocate of Scotland, "Are you aware
Mr. Bagster you are acting contrary to etiquette in wearing
gloves, only military officers wear them. If you have any
doubt of the correctness of this point, I will introduce you
to Sir P. Molyneux, the Master of the Ceremonies." I
heartily thanked his lordship and put a fine pair of gloves
that I had received as a marriage present, rather ignobly,
into my small clothes for my court-dress had not a pocket.

On the night between the first and second day of March,
1822, the awful fire took place which destroyed my
business premises in Paternoster Row and consumed
my stock and I being inefficiently insured suffered a most
intense loss. The horrors of the scene when it first met my
view is not to be described. It flashed on my sight when on
the other side of St. Paul's, making the dome glow with
the light. I then resided at St. Peter's Hill Doctors
Commons and on the dire alarm I retained presence of

mind enough to secure a light in a lantern to enable me to get below, were it possible to save the stereotype plates which were in vaults under the shop, by shutting the iron doors if they should have been left open. On my arrival the stairs above were burning furiously and the flames fearfully increasing and the stairs to the cellar partly, but my Samuel dropped into the basement floor and finding the two iron doors shut, in the hurry of mind the circumstances created, actually opened them. I was as much lost as my dear son, I entreated standers by to get me a light to go down, when I had really brought a lighted candle in a lantern with me—Samuel having thus as he and I supposed done all that could be done below. I wished to get into the front room of the first floor but I could not by the stairs, they being nearly consumed, I endeavoured to get in by the window but it was with much difficulty for the closed shutters denied me entrance. An active sailor, seeing my ineffectual attempts to enter, followed me up the ladder and with an energetic bang with his heels, burst the shutters open. The anxiety I felt to enter that room was strong, lest the Deeds of Mr. Idle's great estates should be destroyed. I had the preceding day directed my clerk to bring them up from the strong room and spread them before the fire to remove the dampness of them. On my entrance I found them spread out; speedily I put them into the several deed-boxes and the deal boxes and happily they were not too large for me to throw them one by one to a person below, who offered to catch them: he did so successfully; except one, all were carried into a neighbour's house and not one of these valuable deeds was lost, or materially injured. One of the deal boxes was carried off by a rogue expecting he had a treasure—this box however contained surveys, etc., and the loss would have produced inconvenience but no actual injury. A gentleman on Ludgate Hill seeing the conflagration and a man running with a box, seized him by the collar and compelled him to come back to the scene of destruction. The box was claimed by me and thus not one was lost! The saving of these important deeds was attended with much danger, the room in which I was, was already half burned. I took care so to stand and move about, as never to tread on any part of a partly burnt joist, lest it sinking with my weight would carry me down with it. I felt a degree of security because the draft of air entering by the opened window encouraged the flames upward, driving the smoke from me. My hat fell off and I could not recover it. This happy direction of the wind that enabled Samuel to drop into the cellar without great danger. The wind which was very high at times, blew from the S.W. carried part of the burnt paper to Hackney and a friend living there picked up a piece that morning in his garden and went into his family and told them Mr. Bagster's house must be burnt, he knowing the leaf to be one of my publications. As soon as the salvation of these deeds of Mr. Idle's estate was secured, I lost my tone of mind and sank into timorousness of spirit. The next morning I was much cheered by a visit from Sir J. W. Lubbock who said, "keep up your confidence, I will give you needful assistance." This was a most kind act and encouraging to me, it had its full effect.

An enquiry by my reader to learn the cause of the fire shall have all the satisfaction that the knowledge of the fact enables me to give. Several months before this destruction we had a warning of danger. On entering the house there was a smell of a wood fire; I went into every room on the premises and, as each one of my people came, they did the same, and we all were of one opinion, that the smell prevailed most in the middle room of the first floor in which there had been no fire and it was almost a solid body of books stacked. The existence of a fire some-where could not be doubted. I sent a statement of the facts to the insurance office; they sent a person who directed the whole bulk of books to be removed to get access to the fireplace. In moving the bundles, I thought there was a slight discolouration on the edge of some of the bundles. The fireman directed a chimney sweeper to be sent for, the boy ascended and had not proceeded up high before he called out with glee, "I've got it" and brought down a lump of burning soot and then he removed a considerable quantity. The fireman said it was all right and perfectly secure but I, desiring to make unquestion-ably secure for the time to come as no fire was needed in that room, directed Place, the blacksmith, to fit an iron plate into the flue of the chimney, whereby no soot could come down, burn or smoke to injure the books, and if soot again gathered and ignited, it might harmlessly burn itself out. This precaution of mine probably caused the very evil it was intended to prevent, this iron plate prevented the possibility of a notice of danger by smelling the fire. After the ruins were somewhat cleared, we found out that the flue of the lower fireplace was brought into this flue, so that thence one flue carried up the smoke from both chimneys. At this union of flues a strong block of wood is placed, technically called discharging piece, and this was burnt almost through and the wainscoting of the room being fastened thereto, took fire and general ruin followed. Had this piece of wood been entirely consumed it would not have been possible to have discovered the cause of the fire. The description of the first observers was confirmatory of this opinion and I continue to receive it as the fact—The Sun Fire office treasurer paid me, it was with sympathy and grace—"I wish, Sir, we had more to pay you towards your loss." The few books of salvage were bought in a most friendly manner. The mass of burnt paper which was taken out when the fire was extinguished were piled up in the square W of my house and sold to Mr. Chidley for £140—it was estimated as weighing twenty tons. The ashes in the basement which had received the metal type, etc., I sold to a metal dealer for a large sum.

Most distressingly long it was before I could come to terms with my landlord for a new and extended lease. He had insured the house and I had insured it also in £500 intending my interest therein and fixtures. This sum the landlord demanded alleging that I had insured the house, instead of insuring the fixtures and my interest in the house. To this overreaching claim and legal quibble he long persevered but happily I discovered a case exactly in point reported in Atkyns, and the result was distinctly in my favour. The Sadler's Company made such a claim against a tenant and were defeated and Lord Hardwick's judgment is given at great length. The exhibition of this case to my landlord, the difficulties were mainly overcome and a compromise soon followed.

Through the effect of this woeful fire I sank in my spirits and became melancholic and one day I felt unusual depression. At the time of this depression I was at the end of the shop and sank into a gloomy reverie, when the door opened and a young man entered. The desponding train of feeling was so intense that I stood still, without advancing to the person. He came up to me and with grace of manner, put a printed handbill into my hand which was headed in large back handed, as MS.

## DON'T DESPAIR

which two words were so large as to fill one sixth of the

bill. The effect was marvellous and beneficial, broke the mental spell, burst the clouds of despair and light entered. My mind was restored to healthy and correct reflection and communicated abiding influences whereby serenity was restored.

The effect of this calamity nevertheless on my whole frame made it necessary that I should for some period quit business and by new scenes recover my wonted tone of health. I had a return of supposed pulmonary symptoms and my medical adviser Mr. Chevalier said a visit to France was necessary and it was approved and took place in August, 1823.

I left London by the river in a steamer: speaking lightly of running aground on the Goodwin Sands (sufficiently alarming at the time), and my dear wife's sharp indisposition by usual sickness, we arrived safely and comfortably on shore at Calais. We made up our minds to travel circuitously to the metropolis, by Dieppe and Rouen, which was done and from the last named place we reached there, travelling the lower road, it being more pleasant and skirting the meandering Seine. The chief of the journey was through such dense clouds of dust as I never before beheld, the scenes however were so novel and the manner of travelling so strange, that it kept me so thoroughly intent on the present, as to feel a strong interest in all that passed and I was refreshed and looked on the future with brighter anticipations. The use of seven horses with a single rein and principally by the voice of the driver, surprised and pleased me much. At Rouen we visited the spot of the cruel execution of the Maid of Orleans, in the old market place where is a figure of her in male attire with a sword and armed cap a pie. The block on which the figure stands is used as a fountain and there flows a continued supply of water. Joan of

Arc, is the most celebrated heroine of history. She is called the Maid of Orleans by her wondrous success in repelling the English then besieging that city. The French were excited by having an inspired leader and the English were as much dismayed. The English raised the siege. She then declared her divine mission as ended and said she would retire into private life, but the French commander induced her to enter Compaigne, then besieged by the English and after performing dauntless wonders of courage, she was taken prisoner when heading a valorous sally against the besiegers. The heroine was carried to Rouen and there tried for sorcery and on this charge was declared guilty, and the English condemned her to be burnt alive and she was carried to the stake and died with heroism on the 30th May, 1431, aged nineteen years.*

As our stay in France was to be but three weeks altogether we made the best of our way to Paris. Our proceedings in the gay city of this volatile people, I will not enter into, as my dear wife has written an interesting journal of the trip, except to notice that the fete of St. Louis called forth a brilliant display of Paris gaiety and such was the beneficial effect of the transparent climate on me, I became so buoyant in my physical energy that I was more ready to vault, skip and fly than walk like a sedate Englishman.

From Paris we stretched our tour to Belgium and Holland. As we entered the Belgian territory from the Paris road, the passengers in the diligence by which we were travelling were ordered to alight; the object was that the Belgian duoniers might examine the baggage and charge the duties on importation on such goods as were so chargeable. The duonier asked me, "Do you declare

* Robert Southey has done poetical justice to the Heroine, which will well please the reader, it delighted me.

anything as chargeable to the Custom duties?" I replied,
"I do not know what is chargeable" and gave him the keys
of my boxes. He opened the trunk and took out the
*Common Prayer in eight Languages*, a pocket volume and
asked if I printed it. I pointed to my name at the foot of
the title page. With a polite bow of the head he looked
at the book attentively, put it again into the trunk and
said he would look no further at the luggage of the owner
of that book. I felt the compliment and being then at
liberty, we prowled about to see all we could. Beneath a
large shed, a vast heap of dutch round cheeses were piled
for import into France and by the heap a man was busy
with a long stiletto piercing through every cheese, lest
lace or other contraband might be ingeniously hidden.
While we were waiting, a gentleman of noble figure in a
most handsome travelling carriage drove up in style and
two ladies were in the carriage—he was seated on the
dicky. He was asked, "What do you declare?" "I declare
on the two candelabra at my feet in this packing case."
They gave not credit to his declaration of these only, but
said, "the ladies must come out that I may examine the
carriage," and it was found the carriage boot seat and
linings were ransacked, a number of contraband articles
were found and we left him in the midst of his mortification and loss. He bore the awkward position with a flushed
face but the ladies were painfully agitated. While we were
at dinner we saw him pass and concluded he had made
some compromise with the authorities.

Our arrival at Brussels was about eleven at night and
the passengers alighted at the proprietor's yard, not at an
inn, and we had to find a lodging, which was not done
without much difficulty, and, at length we found a lodging
on the ground floor of an inn. On the following day we
traversed the city and hired a fiacre and on alighting at our

inn, the charge of the driver was enormous. We objected
and made an appeal to our hostess; she refused to inter-
fere. There was at the altercation a military officer standing by us, observant of the affair. He stepped forward and
said to the driver, "Your fare is only so many francs and
if you do not take it you shall go to the court." The driver
was silenced. I paid him more than the officer named and
then saved considerably. I turned and expressed my
thanks to the officer—he received it not, but with a fierce
countenance and in a furious disdainful manner he
cursed the English and added, "but I will not see even an
Englishman be imposed on." One Sunday as I was
prowling through the city we went into a church to hear
mass, soon after a company of soldiers arrived, as for
parade, with colours and martial music, in military array,
they marched up the broad aisle with the music in full
band. The service was but a few minutes, the priest had
his back to the soldiers speaking in Latin in an indistinct
manner, so that not one word was heard. As soon as it was
finished the command to march was given, the military
music commenced and the men went out in military
order, five abreast and we followed in their rear. My
good wife and I returned discomforted at such mockery
of God. My wife staid in the rest of the day, I proceeded
and roamed farther and went into a large place of worship
as plain as a dissenting meeting-house of the old Presby-
terians in London. The congregation was chiefly soldiers.
I walked up the centre aisle until I was nearly opposite
the pulpit, near to a large square pew of ladies and
gentlemen. After the sermon was finished the congregation
sang and a gentleman in the pew, near which I stood,
came to the front of the pew and sang in a manner that
proved he had sound lungs and did not spare them. The
service was soon over after my entrance and the said

gentleman and those in his pew came down the aisle and all the soldiers arose and faced him. I was directly at their heels. At the door was a splendid carriage and this self same gentleman threw his arms over the shoulders of a lady, kissed her and with apparent ardour as Shakespeare says in "Measure for Measure"—

> "This done, he took the bride about the neck
> And kist her lips with a clamorous smack,
> That at the parting the church did echo."

and helped into the carriage, walking away himself with a young gentleman. These proved to be the King and Queen of the Netherlands.

On Monday we visited Quatre Bras and Waterloo Plain, saw the burial place of the officers slain and of the limb of the Marquess of Anglesea, who was wounded in the thigh and was amputated. The Marquess received his wound when making a dash at Buonaparte's person when reconnoitring the field of battle.

From Brussels we went on to Amsterdam to visit Augustus Birch, my brother-in-law, and his wife. In one part of my excursion was I more pleased than in crossing a wide branch of the Zuder Zea, it was a brilliant night, the moon in her splendour, the passage took about an hour. When we reached the opposite shore, it was about three in the morning and with others we went into a suttler's house where a woman was distributing small pieces of beef, temptingly broiled and each put on a piece of bread. We both had some and surely except honest Trender's potato pie, the annual apple pie at school and the turnip I eat in 1814 at Hanson Toot was so delicious to my palate. In good time of day we arrived at the metropolis of Holland, having passed through Haarlem and the Hague; of both these places I will be silent as my clever wife's pen has given an account of this trip to which my children have willing access.

As soon as out of the carriage I left my good wife in charge of the luggage, while I endeavoured to find my way to Augustus and having but a muddy comprehension of the residence, it being at an Inn which has "The Bible" as its sign. I enquired of a passer by for the said inn; he not understanding me, applied to others and ere long a *very considerable* number of persons were gathered around me, all willing but none able to help, for not one knew English or French better than I knew Dutch. After some discussion they were satisfied of my want, that I was seeking for a lodging and one kind Samaritan was ready. An end was put to the matter by my returning to the office where the Diligence had stopped. I procured a guide and found Mr. Birch's dwelling place was a large room or rooms at the edge (but much *below* the level) of one of the salt water stagnant canals which issue forth unsavoury odours, which to me was so deleterious that the vigour gained by the clear atmosphere of France was nearly lost to me. I actually felt ill by a difficulty to breathe by the heavy-laden atmosphere—full of nauseous effluvia. We therefore hastened from Holland as quickly as we could. I consider that had I remained there a few days I should not have been benefited at all by my French visit. Mightily was I surprised at the countless number of windmills, in one place I could count nearly thirty. The use of these numerous windmills is of essential importance. The meadows are below the sea level, land conquered from the ocean by the industry of man. Nearly every meadow is surrounded with a ditch and the meadows are in a set form, the ditches on the four sides, wide and deep and these mills raise the water from these ditches to the level of the public road, from whence the water is conveyed to the ocean. The fertility of this land is such that successive crops are taken without manuring it. For the account of the Allee verd and the palace and the head quarters of the conquering hero I refer to my dear wife's narrative, but the genteel villas on both sides of the canal, down which we travelled, with their gardens extending to the water I speak of, because my wife was too much overcome with sleep to make it possible to create an interest in the scene. These gentlemanly detached residences were in a line for a few miles from the clean beauteous Hague, at times the capital of Holland. I regret that no opportunity offered of viewing the Hague for from what I did see of it, I consider no city surpasses it in palatial buildings and wide and clean streets. My opinion of Holland generally however may be shortly expressed by saying I disliked it beyond any place I have ever visited and my surprise is great, the lives of Hollanders is not much below the common duration of human existence.

After an absence of little more than three weeks we came to our dear native land, at the custom house I was teased by the duty claimed on a paltry map lent to me by Mr. Chevalier worth about 1/6 or 2/- which was cut into seven pieces, there being seven provinces, each bit they called a whole map and demanded 2/6d on each of the seven pieces, which, as I refused to pay, they retained.

My journey from Dover to London was a rich treat, the enclosed verdant meadows with bordered hedges and richly studded with populous hamlets, was such a contrast to the open fields and scattered inhabitants of France and the dreary ditchery of Holland. England had new charms, but, nevertheless, this short excursion from my country led me to notice and forces me to acknowledge that in many arts, foreigners surpass my countrymen.

On my return from France to which country I went as

I have said to recruit my health and refresh my mind after the calamity of the fire, my eldest son suggested the plan, as his wish, that he might become a printer and I acceded to his wish. A house was taken in Bartholomew Close and while repairing it a fire took place at a book binders very near. The flakes of burning wood flew over the house of my son and many dropped into the yard wherein were wood shavings. I saw a flake go down the chimney, into the next house *beyond* and soon I observed the room on fire. I ran and with little difficulty put it out. This fire happened in the early morning and returning with my dear wife thankful that we had escaped, though in danger from *both* sides. I picked up a morsel of burned paper and on it the words, "His will to accomplish to save or consume us." *My* house was burned, my son's house was not. I believe my daughter Eunice has preserved the piece of paper.

*1825.* My dear mother* had now survived my father six years, they had been calm and peaceful years to her but she never ceased to mourn my father's loss and often to say she wished she was in her little narrow house with her dear George. One of her family was always with her— my dear wife, my sister Mary or my niece Anne, but domestic claims often prevented them from leaving home, and so my daughter Eunice who had no duties to call her away, almost entirely resided with her grandmama, during the latter years of her life. My dear mother had much comfort in her man servant, he had become a pious and consistent character while under her roof and now her age and infirmities increased and her deafness rendered reading to her difficult. He used to read the Bible and pray by her side and when at last confined to her bed she could not miss Robert's prayers, he used to bend over and

* She died November, 1823. W.B.

pray into her ear. After his mistress died he married his fellow servant and when last I heard of them they were happy and prosperous. Old Hetty was still living and became the care of my niece Anne, who, as her father's housekeeper, became mistress of the house in which my parents lived at St. Pancras, after her grandmother's death.

It was in this year 1825 my son Samuel's marriage took place on 22nd June. His wife Elizabeth was the daughter of Mr. and Mrs. Atlee Hunt of Harmondsworth near Hounslow. Since my son's decease she married Mr. Simon Saunders, a bookseller of Conduit Street, Hanover Square. My dear son who died on July 1st, 1835, was buried in the family vault of Mr. Birch in Tottenham Court Chapel but on my purchase of a burial place for myself and family in the Abney Cemetery, Stamford Hill, I removed his body to it that our dust might lie together until the ressurrection summons.

# 1828 - 1835

The ninth Septennial Division of my life—1828 to 1835, being the fifty-sixth to sixty-third year of my age.

As I began the former division of my days, by noticing my introduction to George IV by the Archbishop of Canterbury (Sutton) to present the Book of Common Prayer in eight languages, I will commence the present era by stating my introduction to William IV by the then Archbishop of Canterbury (Howley). That amiable prelate made the appointment for me to meet him at his residence in Whitehall Gardens and accompany him to be presented at the private entree. My next door neighbour Alderman Kelly lent me his chariot and servants, of very handsome style. His Grace asked whether I would like best to ride with him or in my own carriage; I preferred of course the honour of riding with him and my carriage followed and staid in the innercourt to take me home after my presentation. A very short period I had to wait in the anti-room when His Grace came to accompany me to the presence of His Majesty and seeing I was lame, the mild Primate courteously insisted on carrying the folio Polyglott Bibles for me, an act of considerate kindness I shall long remember. I was introduced to the king in the most impressive manner. King William in his person and bearing did not evidence, like his brother the late monarch, features of dignity and royal deportment, by no means, he was frank and abrupt and seemed glad to hasten over the ceremonies. The anti-chamber in which I was waiting is used for those persons to meet who possess the privilege of the private entrance and amongst others was Don Pedro, the emperor of Brazil. He was decorated with a broad rich green ribbon which he wore in the manner of the Knights of the Garter.

My dear son John, who had all his life had a predilection for farming and had served seven years to qualify himself for that occupation, in 1829 took possession of a farm at Coleshill near Amersham and my daughter Eunice, became his housekeeper.

*1828.* I adopted what I considered the best method to ascertain the value of farms, I employed a friend on whom I relied to give his opinion of each one as it was offered. We had been cautiously looking out for several years and we hoped the choice of this might be all we desired,—it proved to be otherwise. The land was poor and exhausted by the preceding worthless tenant and my poor son had only sorrow and vexation connected with it, his health was broken and his spirits gave way.

The year 1830 was distinguished by the repeal of the Test Act, whereby the right for Dissenters to hold office was established. The event was carried after long and very violent debates.

In 1832 our relations the Dentons were horrified by the atrocious murder of Mr. Paas, the brother of Mrs. Samuel Denton. Mr. Paas was a tool-cutter and he called on business on a bookbinder of the name of Smith in Nottingham to receive payment of his bill for tools he had supplied. Mr. Paas in the presence of Mr. Smith in his workshop opened his bill and money case, which it is supposed caused in Smith's mind the culpable intention to murder him to possess the contents. He committed the murder and then to hide his guilt took the monstrous course of hiding the crime by destruction of the body by boiling and burning it. He was however discovered by the stinking effluvia and was hanged.

This year 1832, on August 1st, my dear Augusta was married to Mr. Alfred Holloway, and this year we in the family playfully call it the marrying year.

My daughter and Mr. Holloway as above stated.

My cousin Martha Rowles to Mr. James Smith.

Mr. Holloway's sister Arabella to Mr. Goodman.

My niece Anne Bagster to Mr. Toms.

My niece Mary Prosser married to my nephew William Bagster.

My nephew Joseph Bagster to Miss Burls.

My nephew Joseph Mossett to Mary Yoanna Shirley.

Miss Sophia Marks to Rev. Mr. Vine.

My daughter Charlotte was this year three times to bare the honour of Bride's maid; to her sister Augusta, Mrs. Joseph Bagster and her friend Sophia Marks.

In December of 1832 and the January of 1833 I was seized with violent illness. I consider the danger that attended it chiefly arising from my taking too strong a dose of purgative. My medical adviser, was Mr. Thomas Chevalier Junr. who gave medicine which failing in affording relief, he prescribed an electuary of which I was directed to take the quantity of a nutmeg, but my dear wife states that I exceeded that quantity. Be that as it may, the effect was direful, the diarrhoea was dangerously severe and threatened to end my life. The effect was paralysis of the lower part of my body, a lifelessness in the limbs and long it was before I recovered but which I have not entirely, having ever since suffered by lameness. There was a consultation on my case by S. Farre, Sir Charles Bell, and Mr. Thomas Chevalier, the consultation was I consider of little advantage to me. Indeed it was nearly proving injurious for the doctors being unaware of the high pulse natural to me and judging by my buoyancy of spirits when I discoursed with them were about to direct bleeding, but my wife who better knew my constitution interfered and saved me. In that severe illness I was visited by two young friends, Mr. William Greenfield and Mr. John Webb and my dear son Samuel, the whole three were about thirty years of age and in fine sound health. Their visit was as a farewell visit, a final interview with two, but inscrutable are God's appointment and such the uncertainty of human existence, all, within a few years removed by death in the noon of life, while I am here seventeen years after in health, and may yet longer live.

After this illness I revisited France, now not only with my dear wife but also with my two unmarried daughters, Eunice and Charlotte. Our tour was confined to Normandy and France not extending to Belgium and Holland. We met a very agreeable gentleman at the hotel at Calais who with his pupil Master Boucher were taking like ourselves a peep at France. Their intention was to return immediately home, as they had merely run over from Dover but the tutor feeling confidence in us and Master Boucher wishing much to see Paris, proposed that he should proceed to Paris with us. On account of my infirmity and the responsibility of the charge we felt compelled to decline; they returned and we proceeded on our journey. We were about three weeks in France and the trip as before did my general health good but my lameness was not lessened but my health being better I was able with a stick to walk four miles at a stretch. Age with its increasing weakness has brought me to what I am now, 1849, but yet with help I can yet walk a short distance. I have a horse and carriage to ride abroad, a garden chair to use therein and indoors by the aid of castors to my sitting chair, I am conveniently drawn from room to room and so with infirmities I have valuable alleviations and many blessings and my spirits are as buoyant as in boyhood.

# 1835 - 1842

The tenth Septennial Era—1835 to 1842. The sixty-fourth to the seventieth year of my age.

Having now passed the grand climacteric being sixty-four years of age, which—

> Those in health, who are but seldom sick
>     Much dread—'tis called the great climacteric.
> E'en Pliny full of boding fear,
>     Depicts this year a dangerous year,
> And says—"But reach to sixty-four,
>     Hope have you then, for many more."

In 1835 my son John gave up his farm. I had given him the offer to return to take a share in my business which he accepted. At that time my son Samuel was very ill. The illness had gradually come on him the preceding year but it assumed in January, 1835, an alarming aspect. Mr. Frogley his medical adviser wished to consult Sir Benjamin Brodie and my son who resided at Shepherd's Bush went with him in his own carriage for that purpose. The opinion of Sir Benjamin Brodie was decided and my dear son in the evening of the day in which he heard it, wrote to me, "I shall be in Heaven before you." It was sound good hope beyond the grave that enabled my dear son thus calmly to look at death. This consultation and decision was on January 6th, the day after my son John and Eunice quitted the farm. Samuel lingered in much suffering to July 1st when he expired. He left a widow but no child.

In the year 1836 my dear daughter, Charlotte, married

Mr. R. H. C. Tims, only son of Mr. Tims bookseller of Dublin and in the year 1837 my dear son Jonathan married Nancy Horsey Toms, daughter of Mr. John Toms, bookseller of Chard, Somerset.

Since my retirement from business and residence in Old Windsor and consequent leisure, I have been open to embrace a view, and examination of curious scenes around my home; we visit Cooper's Hill to give a zest to the perusal of Sir John Denham's epic poem, who sings—

### COOPER'S HILL

"My eye descending from the hill, surveys
Where Thames among the wanton vallies strays.
Thames, the most lov'd of all the Ocean's sons
By his old sire, to his embraces runs;
Hasting to pay his tribute to the Sea,
Like mortal life to meet eternity.
O would I flow like thee, and make they stream
My great example, as it is my theme!
Though deep, yet clear, though gentle, yet not dull,
Strong without rage, without o'erflowing full."

Below this hill, to which Denham's muse has brought abiding renown Runny mede spreads its plain, where the Charter of British Liberty was signed.

Sir John Denham sings—

"Here was that Charter seal'd, wherein the crown
All marks of arbitrary power lays down;
Tyrant and Slave, those names of hate and fear,
The happier style of King and Subject bear;
Happy, when both to the same centre move,
When Kings give Liberty, and subjects Love."

Surely not one of my gentle readers will fail to recall to mind the strain of Britain's moral poet—

"'Tis Liberty alone that gives the flower
  Of fleeting life its lustre and perfume,
  And we are weeds without it."

In commemoration of this all important event Mr. Harcourt whose property embraces the reputed spot, has built a fishing house on the site. Visitors are allowed the privilege to enter the house; the principal room has a fac simile of Magna Charta framed and glazed and the panels of the room are emblazoned with the armorial bearings of the bold barons who demanded and obtained this Charter and the Charta Forest, also mighty importance to the British nation.

Some beautiful lines in the form of a sonnet which we picked up on a scrap of paper, are worthy of transcription and remembrance; my readers may know the author but I do not. My daughter Eunice often repeats it when passing over "The Mead"—

"Fair Runnymede! oft hath my lingering eye,
  Paused on thy tufted green and grassy hill
  And there my busy soul would drink her fill
  Of lofty dreams which on thy bosom lie.
  There dost not need a perishable stone of sculptured story,
  Records ever young proclaim the gladdening triumph thou
                                                    hast won,
  The soil, the passing stream, have still a tongue,
  And ev'ry wind breathes out an el'quent strain
  That FREEDOM'S self might wake thy fields among."

Amongst other interesting scenes in my circle of visits I will name my visit to the ancient Church of Bray, which on account of the poetical record of the versatility of one of its vicars is become familiar to English ears: few songs won such wide popularity. This vicar of Bray lived in "Good King Charles' golden days", "When Royal James obtained the crown", "When William was our king declar'd", "When gracious Anne became our Queen", "When George in pudding time came o'er".

> For on my faith and loyalty
> I never more will falter,
> And George my lawful king shall be
> Until the times do alter.

The Chorus:

> And this is law, I will maintain
> Until my dying day, Sir!
> That whatever king shall reign
> I'll be the Vicar of Bray, Sir!

Not because the character of the Vicar of Bray has been painted by a wit, did I go to see the ancient church but because I was informed that in that church one of the bibles was still chained to the reading desk as directed by Henry VIII. One residing on the skirt of the burial ground obtained the keys, as he opened the ponderous venerable door, assured me the report was true, a bible was really chained. As I walked up the aisle I felt much interest by viewing the brass escutcheons on the treadway, sepulchral memorials of the dignitaries whose dust lay beneath. After gazing on these memorials of clerical grandeur which walking over them has so much obliterated, I may say now illegible, I went to see the chained relic, but to my disappointment and surprise, the reputed Bible was only an early edition of Fox's book of the Martyrs printed in old English type.

This book brings forth the pleasing fact, although the sepulchres are of papal rank in the church the pulpit has protestant light.

The brazen remains of the pompous dust in Bray Church, I leave in their foot-worn glory to notice the existence of a humbler class of claimants for long remembrance. I allude to the epitaphs written by well-meaning persons who intends to be impressively pathetic and awaken a sympathy of feeling towards the departed, but which only raise a gentle smile. There is an example in point in my parish church of Old Windsor on the south side of the church, near the path leading to the entrance door.

It is a wooden memorial of the common form and has an inscription on the two sides, the one by the husband who first dies, the other by the wife who dies some years after; and, it is so quaint it should be preserved, that the *precious* lines may be kept in remembrance longer, I copy the inscription into my pages. The wood has already gone much to decay and the names of this dear loving pair are by time effaced, if I knew it, I would do them honour—

> Haste my dear wife and follow me,
> On earth you cannot happy be;
> Though long we toil'd in grief and pain,
> In bliss let's hope to meet again.

The wife lives some years longer and she replies—

> Dear Husband! I be come,
> To lie by you in a cold tomb,
> Our parting it was great grief,
> I hope Christ will give us relief:
> I pray'd for it night and day,
> The time was long, that I did stay.

# 1842 - 1849

The eleventh Septenary Division of my life—1842 to 1849 —from seventy to seventy-nine years of age.

Having fulfilled the desire of my dear wife and daughter so far as to the end of the tenth era of my life, in doing which I have had frequent misgivings as to the propriety of my acquiescence with their request; that is beyond a remedy, but this I consider certain, that on a persual, many things are in I might wish excluded and some omitted I shall wish to have been preferred, and likely such perusal shall cause regret of this use of my pen altogether.

In the writing of these reminiscences there has been a commixture of feeling—burdensome, yet relieved by the pleasure of my compliance with the loving request; and hours occupied that might have been employed less interestingly. One remark it is needful to make, that, as the narrative is the outflow of present memory, without any previous intention or preparation, there will be seen many deficiencies and possibly some errors of date or minutio of detail. Therefore, let it be read merely as a transcript from the page of my memory and if any error has crept in the reader not to question my intention to be exact, but to attribute such error to the mistakes or escapes of mental recollection.